CUT
AND
RUN

Books by Fern Michaels

Spirit of the Season
Deep Harbor
Fate & Fortune
Sweet Vengeance
Holly and Ivy
Fancy Dancer
No Safe Secret
Wishes for Christmas
About Face
Perfect Match
A Family Affair
Forget Me Not
The Blossom Sisters
Balancing Act
Tuesday's Child
Betrayal
Southern Comfort
To Taste the Wine
Sins of the Flesh
Sins of Omission
Return to Sender
Mr. and Miss
Anonymous
Up Close and Personal
Fool Me Once
Picture Perfect
The Future Scrolls
Kentucky Sunrise
Kentucky Heat

Kentucky Rich
Plain Jane
Charming Lily
What You Wish For
The Guest List
Listen to Your Heart
Celebration
Yesterday
Finders Keepers
Annie's Rainbow
Sara's Song
Vegas Sunrise
Vegas Heat
Vegas Rich
Whitefire
Wish List
Dear Emily
Christmas at
Timberwoods

The Sisterhood Novels

Cut and Run
Safe and Sound
Need to Know
Crash and Burn
Point Blank
In Plain Sight
Eyes Only

FERN MICHAELS

CUT
AND
RUN

ZEBRA BOOKS
KENSINGTON PUBLISHING CORP.
www.kensingtonbooks.com

ZEBRA BOOKS are published by

Kensington Publishing Corp.
119 West 40th Street
New York, NY 10018

All Kensington titles, imprints, and distributed lines are available at special quantity discounts for bulk purchases for sales promotion, premiums, fund-raising, educational, or institutional use.

Special book excerpts or customized printings can also be created to fit specific needs. For details, write or phone the office of the Kensington Sales Manager: Attn.: Sales Department. Kensington Publishing Corp., 119 West 40th Street, New York, NY 10018. Phone: 1-800-221-2647.

First Kensington Books Hardcover Printing: September 2019
First Zebra Books Mass-Market Paperback Printing: January 2020
ISBN-13: 978-1-4201-4604-2
ISBN-10: 1-4201-4604-1

ISBN-13: 978-1-4201-4605-9 (eBook)
ISBN-10: 1-4201-4605-X (eBook)

10 9 8 7 6 5 4 3 2 1

Printed in the United States of America

Books by Fern Michaels (cont.)

Anthologies

A Snowy Little Christmas

Coming Home for Christmas

A Season to Celebrate

Mistletoe Magic

Winter Wishes

The Most Wonderful Time

When the Snow Falls

Secret Santa

A Winter Wonderland

I'll Be Home for Christmas

Making Spirits Bright

Holiday Magic

Snow Angels

Silver Bells

Comfort and Joy

Sugar and Spice

Let It Snow

A Gift of Joy

Five Golden Rings

Deck the Halls

Jingle All the Way

Published by Kensington Publishing Corporation

Dear Readers,

Today is a WOW day, but first things first and then we'll get to the WOW part . . .

So many people have asked me over the years how I get fresh ideas this many books into a series. I don't think any of my colleagues (okay, okay, two of my colleagues who are also close friends) will mind if I share that some writers have a few quirky habits. One of mine is that I do a handmade drawing on a piece of plain white paper and tape it to my bedroom door. It's a drawing of the book I'm currently working on with a number next to it. It's the last thing I see before lights out and the first thing I see when the lights go on in the morning. Makes me feel all kinds of warm and fuzzy knowing I dreamed all night about what I plan to work on today. Now, don't go thinking I'm a genius here. Most times I can't remember what I dreamed anyway. It's mostly just for fun.

I loved writing this book because I love Spain. I was fortunate to visit Barcelona and many small towns and villages years and years ago. The people were so warm and gracious, and they all wanted to feed me, to fatten me up. They would laugh and smile and say how skinny I was. Ha! That was then, this is now. I weigh a wee bit more than the 98 pounds I was back then. And just for the record, upon my return I weighed 102 when I set foot on American soil.

Many of the places I described in the book are real, but I'm sure some of my memories are not as accurate as they were back then. I loved the old monastery. If I close my eyes I can smell the beeswax candles and incense, and I have a clear vision of the pure beauty of everything I could see, touch, and smell. Back then I thought of it as an ethereal place like no other I had ever seen for some reason. I hope after you finish the book you will put Spain on your "to visit someday" list.

Here's the WOW! I want you all to know that I was astonished when I realized the number I mentioned earlier, written next to the inspiration for this book, was thirty. *Cut and Run* is the thirtieth book in the Sisterhood series! Who knew??? Not me, that's for sure. I thought maybe one, possibly two, or even three books for a trilogy! Never in a million years did I think in terms of double digits. And I never could have imagined a spin-off series, the Men of the Sisterhood, featuring the guys—a series that, by the way, I love, love, love writing. Harry and Jack are just too cool.

Here's the thing, people. I couldn't have done it without you. Thank you a million times over.

This WOW is for all of you!!!!!!!!

Fern

Prologue

Countess Anna Ryland de Silva's eyes snapped open as if they were spring-loaded. She was instantly wide-awake, wondering what had roused her. She looked over at Fergus, who was sleeping peacefully. Her gaze went to the security alarm by the bedroom door. It glowed bright green. Green meant that the house was safe from intruders. She looked over at the window to see if one of the low-hanging limbs from the oak outside had brushed against the window. The moonlight outlined the leafless tree limbs. There was no wind, no breeze of any kind.

Something's not right.

Annie, as she was known to all those she held dear, swung her legs over the side of the bed, her eyes on the red digital numbers on her bedside clock: 3:17 AM. She reached for her ancient ratty bathrobe, which had to be at least forty years old and was like an old friend. Fergus constantly teased her about the robe, which had been laundered thousands of times. She had shut him down immediately when she said she would sooner give him up before she'd ever part with her robe. To show him she was serious, she wore her tiara when she plopped his blueberry muffin down on his plate at breakfast time. Fergus never commented on the robe again, not a single time.

Annie's feet slid into her fuzzy yellow slippers, a gift from Fergus one Christmas. She loved them as much as she loved the ratty old bathrobe. She tiptoed from the room and made her way down the stairs to the old farmhouse's kitchen. The first thing she saw was the glowing green light on the alarm by the back door. Safe.

Something's not right.

Annie's heart kicked up a beat, then two.

She made coffee, then went to the kitchen window to stare out at the black night. She clicked on the TV on the kitchen counter, pressing button after button that would allow her to see the security cameras' various views of the house. The motion sensors showed nothing. There were no intruders.

Something's not right.

Her breathing was back to normal as her mind raced. Her thoughts went immediately to Myra, Charles, and the girls. If something was wrong where they were concerned, she would have heard something about it by now.

There was nothing or no one else in her life who would cause her concern. Still, she couldn't shake the feeling that was slowly coming to overwhelm her. She watched the water slowly dripping into the coffeemaker. Maybe by the time she heard the last plop, something would have happened. Such a stupid thought.

What? What? What? her mind screamed silently. She heard the last plop. She poured coffee. Nothing had happened. So much for stupid thoughts.

Annie sat down at the old oak table that Fergus had refinished for her. A treasure to be sure. She stared at the bowl of bright yellow mums in the center of the table. Then her gaze traveled to the old-fashioned wall phone that she loved. At least she could hear on it as opposed to all the newfangled phones that she had to keep saying, "Huh, what did you say again?"

As if on cue, the phone on the wall jangled loudly.

Annie was off her chair faster than if she'd been shot from a cannon. She reached the phone before it could ring a second time. Her voice was raspy, almost a growl of sound, and yet all she'd said was hello.

"Señora de Silva?"

Oh, God!

"Yes, speaking." She waited for the caller to continue.

"This is Padre Diaz. The bishop has assigned me to come here to the mountain to help Padre Mendoza. Since he broke his hip several months ago, he is not nearly as agile as he had been. He asked me to call you because, even with his hearing aids, he has difficulty hearing what is said on the telephone. Transatlantic calls would be worse to his way of thinking."

Something's not right, she thought.

Her instincts were spot-on. "How can I help you, Padre Diaz? Are you aware that it is the middle of the night here in America? What can be so urgent to call now? Is this an emergency of some kind? Is Padre Mendoza all right? What happened?"

"I do not know, señora. I'm just doing what Padre Mendoza asked me to do. I am sorry for calling you in the middle of the night. As to an emergency or urgency, I would have to say it is a possibility even though those words were not said aloud to me."

Annie's tongue felt thick in her mouth. "What . . . What is the message for me, Padre Diaz?"

"The message is, please ask Señora de Silva to come to the mountain as soon as she can. He also said to tell you that the people in the village have blocked the entrance to the mountain. He said you would understand. What do you want me to tell Padre Mendoza, Countess?"

Annie didn't stop to think before she spoke. She owed her life to the aging padre, and she could deny him nothing. Nothing at all. "Tell him I am on my way."

"God have mercy on your travels, Countess. I will relay your response to Padre Mendoza immediately."

Annie replaced the phone receiver on the hook with slow, deliberate movements. She waited till she heard the dial tone, then pressed a series of numbers. "Andrew, this is Anna de Silva. I need you to ready the plane. Wheels up in ninety minutes."

She listened for a moment before saying, "To Barcelona, Spain." She listened again, and said, "One passenger. Just me."

Annie moved then, faster than she'd ever moved in her life. She was dressed in under ten minutes. A bag was packed in under five minutes. She spent a full minute staring down at Fergus, who was still sleeping soundly. She swallowed hard before she once again tiptoed out of the bedroom.

In the kitchen, she turned off the coffee-maker, looked around for her keys and purse and heavy jacket. She took another minute to scrawl a note to Fergus that she propped up against the bright yellow mums in the center of the table.

> *Dearest Fergus,*
> *I have something I have to take care of and must leave for a while. Hold down the fort as they say.*
> *Much love, Annie*

Annie's thoughts were all over the map as she broke every speed law on the books to make it to the private airport where she hangared her Gulfstream. She parked her car and wondered how she could be so out of breath when she'd been sitting the whole time in her quest to get to the airport for the ninety-minute wheels up.

The time was five fifty when the sleek silver Gulfstream roared down the runway and soared into the dark sky.

The lone passenger buckled into the soft, buttery, leather armchair leaned back and finally let the tears flow down her cheeks.

Chapter 1

Three months later

The Christmas Eve dinner Charles and Fergus had spent countless hours preparing, which smelled wonderful and tasted delicious, went mostly uneaten. Even Maggie and Kathryn, both of whom normally ate nonstop, only stirred and moved the food around on their plates. There was no joy, no happy chatter at the festively decorated dining room table as per Christmas Eve dinners in years past. Even the dogs were quietly lying under the table and not begging for tidbits to be slipped to them when no one was looking.

The reason for the glum faces and lack of appetite was the empty chair at the long table. Annie's chair.

"This is the worst Christmas Eve dinner I've

ever attended," Alexis said, a sob catching in her throat.

"It's been three months since we've seen Annie! *Three months!*" Isabelle whispered, but her words were still loud enough for the others to hear because the dining room was as quiet as a tomb.

Charles half rose from his chair, his mouth open, no doubt, to expound about his rule that no such talk was permitted at the table.

Kathryn, the most verbal, with her take-no-prisoners approach to life, and the Sisters' wild card, reared up and said, "Put a cork in it, Charles. How can you expect us to sit here with that empty chair staring at us and not say what we're all thinking? Well?" she demanded, her voice dripping ice and daring him to come up with an explanation that she and the others could tolerate and live with.

Charles threw his hands in the air. "It's Christmas Eve," he said lamely by way of a defense.

"My point exactly," Kathryn said in a tone that stopped just short of being a snarl.

"When are we going to do something? By doing something, I mean trying to find out where Annie is and why she left in the middle of the night. Three months is wayyyy too long for her not to be in touch with any of us, especially Myra," Maggie said.

"She could be in trouble, and we'd never know. This is not the Annie we all know and love," Yoko said. Harry's head bobbed up and down to show he was in agreement with his wife.

All heads turned to Fergus, who did the same thing Charles had done. He threw his hands in the air.

"Annie does not like it when people—and it doesn't matter who it is—stick their nose into her business. You all know that as well as I do. The note she left said she would be in touch. She just didn't give a time or a place *when* that would happen," he said defensively.

"That's not good enough," Nikki said. "I think we should go down to the war room right now, talk this out, and form a plan, a mission if you like that word better, to find Annie. Three months, ninety days, is simply too long for us to believe that nothing is wrong. If I were missing for that long, I would expect the rest of you to be doing everything in your power to make sure that nothing was amiss.

"If Annie turns on us for interfering, that's something we'll have to live with. And I don't care if it's Christmas Eve or not. Something is definitely wrong. I can feel it. That's my personal opinion, to be sure, but I think the rest of you feel the same way I do."

The mad scramble from the table stunned Charles as the Sisters and Brothers beelined from the room. Charles looked at the half-eaten food on Myra's heirloom dinner plates, at the beautiful crimson poinsettia centerpiece, compliments of Yoko and Harry. He turned to Fergus, and carefully said, "Are you certain, Ferg, that you have no clue where Annie might have gone?" It was a question he'd asked hundreds of times since Annie's departure.

Fergus responded the same way he'd responded the previous hundreds of times. "I'm sure, mate. As Jack always says, I did not see this coming. I checked with the airport to see if I could find out where she took the Gulfstream. New York. Once she left there, they must have changed their flight plan. I doubt that even Avery can find out where that plane landed. For all we know, her plane could be hangared at some private airport, and she could have flown commercial to her destination. Knowing Annie, if she doesn't want to be found, she will not be found.

"As of this morning, the Gulfstream has still not returned from wherever it flew. It's the very first thing I check every morning. That plane is wherever she is or stashed somewhere else. Her pilot is off the grid and doesn't answer calls or texts.

"By the way, Charles, I want to thank you again for allowing me to stay here. I would have lost my mind staying at the farm by myself."

"No problem, glad to have you. We need to go down to the war room, Ferg."

Fergus waved his hand over the table as much as to say, what about all of this?

"The hell with it," Charles said, heaving himself up and out of his chair. Fergus blinked but followed suit.

Charles looked around at the chaos in the war room, where Lady Justice prevailed on the monster screen hanging from the rafters. He wished he'd stayed upstairs. From the expression on Ferg's face, it looked as if he felt the same way. It was pure bedlam, with the girls snapping and snarling at one another as they pointed to Annie's empty chair. "Someone needs to sit in *that* chair!" Nikki bellowed.

"That's Annie's chair," Dennis West bleated. "It would be sacrilegious to sit in it!"

When he entered the room and saw what was taking place, Charles let loose a loud, shrill whistle. The room went silent immediately.

"You all sound like a gaggle of squalling cats. All this noise and bedlam will get us nowhere. Let's all quiet down and start acting like the responsible adults we allegedly are," Charles said.

When Charles was satisfied that he had everyone's attention, he cleared his throat. "It is obvious to all of us that we have a crisis on hand with one of our own. And we need to deal with it. I have to wonder, though, why you all waited for tonight, Christmas Eve, to rear up and act like a pack of ten-year-old brats."

"It was the empty chair at dinner, dear," Myra said. "I think it hit all of us at the same time. Annie always loved Christmas."

"Why did you just use the past tense?" Maggie barked. "Do you know something the rest of us don't know? Well?" Maggie barked again.

Myra just shrugged, her face a mask of sadness. "I know what you all know, which is absolutely nothing."

Jack stood up and held up both hands to show he wanted everyone's attention. "Let me start off with saying this. Do not let your emotions cloud the issue. We all feel the same way about Annie. That's a given. We need to think and act like this is a mission. Feelings, no matter how strong they are, have to be set aside. First things first. We all need to recognize and realize that Annie left of her own free will. Second, if she wanted us to know what was going on, she would have called us. She knows that all of us, and I stress all of us, would have stopped whatever we were doing and rushed to her aid. Third, the fact that she did not do that tells us whatever happened is something she considers personal and private, something that she did not want to share with us. I, for one, do not have a clue as to what that would be.

"Fourth, she used subterfuge to keep us from learning where she was going. I'm talking about her private plane. I don't know much about aviation and planes, but I don't think it's all that easy to hide a giant Gulfstream. Which raises the question, why the need to hide the plane?

"Fifth, Annie's pilot and hostess are incommunicado. Obviously on Annie's orders. That tells us that Annie does not want to be found, and she does not want any interference from any of us."

"So, then what are we supposed to do, Jack?" Ted asked.

"That's the sixty-four-thousand-dollar question, isn't it?" Jack growled.

"I don't care what anyone says, three months

is way too long for Annie not to be in touch with us. She loves us all the way we love her. She wouldn't *knowingly* put us through all this angst if she could help it. I believe that heart and soul," Maggie said, passion ringing in her voice. The others agreed by smacking their hands on the table to show their support for Maggie's proposition.

"You're saying we should throw caution to the wind and go full bore, is that what you're saying?" Charles asked. "Even knowing if we're wrong we'll all face Annie's wrath at some point."

"Damn straight," Kathryn said.

Charles's eyes sparked as they settled on his beloved. "Then let's get to it, people. Ferg, call Avery now. Tell him to come here immediately. I know for a fact he's alone even though we invited him for Christmas. He told me that he wanted to sleep through the holiday. He's registered at the Hay-Adams because he likes their Christmas decorations. He can be here in no more than an hour."

"Where should we start?" Nikki asked.

Everyone focused on Myra, who had tears in her eyes.

Charles's voice was sweet and gentle when he said, "Myra, you've known Annie since you were babies in nappies. Tell us about everything you know about Annie. Even if it pains you and you have to share secrets. We need all the help we can get if we're to help her."

* * *

The sun was creeping over the horizon when Myra Rutledge yanked at the zipper on her travel bag. She looked around, not knowing what it was that she was looking for. Charles? She sniffed and smelled the aroma of Charles's special coffee blend wafting up to the second floor. She spun around when she heard her husband enter the bedroom.

"Anything I can do?"

"I wish there was, Charles. Truly I do, but no."

"Can I ask where you're going, old girl?"

Myra smiled ruefully. "The only place I can think of. Spain. The mountain. I should have done this three months ago. Why didn't I, Charles?"

"Because you know Annie better than anyone on earth. You were respecting what you perceived to be her wishes. In so many ways, Annie is a private person, and in so many other ways, she's an open book. You were trying to be the friend you are and always have been. I knew when we went to bed last night that this was what you were going to do. You see, old girl, I know you as well as you know Annie."

"The girls are going to be upset with me," Myra whispered.

"Yes, they will be upset. But, having said that, they will understand. Are you flying first class?"

"No, first class was sold out. It doesn't matter. I booked on short notice, just a few hours ago to be precise. I didn't sleep much last night. Maybe I'll sleep on the flight. I'm scared, Charles," Myra said, stepping into his arms. "Truly I am. What if Annie isn't on the mountain? What if something happened to her, and we never find out? She did say she was never ever going back to the mountain. She was so firm about that.

"Actually, it was more than that. Much more. It was a promise. Annie never ever makes a promise she can't keep. That's why I think she's gone there. She thinks we'll never look there because of that promise. Whatever happened has something to do with that damn mountain. I feel it in every pore of my body. But what if I'm wrong? What if I'm wrong, Charles?" Myra cried, wiping at her eyes.

"Then, my dear, you will deal with it like you deal with everything else. Do you want me to go with you? I can be ready in ten minutes. Fergus can watch the dogs."

Myra squeezed her arms around her husband. "I appreciate the offer, Charles, but this is something I have to do on my own. I'm not sure why that is, it just is."

"Can I at least drive you to the airport?"

"Yes, dear, you can. I was going to take the farm truck and leave it at the long-term lot."

"Let me wake Fergus, and we'll get this show on the road. Do you have time for coffee and a sticky bun? I baked some when I first got up."

Myra looked at her watch. "Sorry, no, we'll be cutting it close as it is. I'll make us both a cup to go. Two sticky buns for you and one for me. I'm so glad you aren't upset with me. I mean, I know you are, and you are just trying to . . . to . . . never mind. I have to do this, that's the bottom line."

"I know, love, I know. Don't fret now. Go down and fix our coffee while I roust Ferg. Now if anyone is going to be upset, it's Ferg. Count on it. I'll fetch your bag."

Myra waved her arm as she rushed to the back stairway that would take her down to the kitchen. Once there, she moved quickly, pouring coffee into two thermos containers and wrapping the sticky buns in wax paper. She took a moment to savor the rich smell of cinnamon before she looked down at the dogs, who were staring up at her as if they knew exactly what was going on.

"I won't be gone too long. This is important and something I have to do. You know I'm leaving you in good hands." Tears blurred Myra's eyes as she bent down to cup Lady's face in her hands. The pups whined softly as they clustered around their mistress's legs for a comforting pat to the head. She did her best to hug them all just as Charles and Fergus galloped down the stairs.

Myra took one look at the misery etched on Fergus's face and wanted to cry. "If she's there, Fergus, I will bring her home. That's a promise."

Fergus licked at his dry lips as his fingers raked through his sparse bed hair. All he could do was nod before he made shooing motions with his hands, indicating they should leave.

Five minutes later, Charles blasted through the gate, which wasn't fully open. He saw Myra flinch as the monster gate scraped the shiny black Mercedes. "It can be fixed, don't worry about it, Charles. I hate to say this, but you're going to have to speed, so be careful. I don't want to miss my flight."

"Trust me, love. I will get you there on time. I've never failed you, have I?" Myra didn't think that statement deserved a reply, so she just stared out the window at the beginning of a new day, a new day she wouldn't be sharing with her husband. She did her best to ignore the tight knot forming in her stomach. *I'm coming, Annie, I'm coming.*

Charles was as good as his word. Myra made her flight with under five minutes to spare. She was one of the last to board the flight. She was breathless and light-headed when she settled into her seat and buckled up. She leaned back and closed her eyes. *I'm coming, Annie. I'm coming.*

Chapter 2

The hostess's voice woke Myra with a start. She blinked and quickly buckled her seat belt. She was here. She blinked again, wondering how she could feel so tired when she had just woken up. Stress. She stifled a yawn, checked her watch, which she had set six hours ahead when she boarded the flight at Reagan National Airport back in D.C.

Myra could feel the plane descending. This was the part of flying that she hated. *I'm coming, Annie. I might not get to you tonight, but by tomorrow we'll be face-to-face.*

Myra wished she'd woken earlier so she could have splashed some cool water on her face. Her skin felt dry and parched. She looked around for the water bottle that had been at her side. It was gone. Obviously the hostess had removed it while she slept. A tired sigh escaped her lips as her gaze dropped to her watch. She'd traveled 4,044 miles. She'd been on this plane for almost nine hours. She'd picked at three meals, nibbled on six snacks and sipped at four tiny bottles of water. Yet she still felt parched. She also itched.

Myra squeezed her eyes shut as the wheels touched down on the runway. She hated this part of any flight just like she hated the actual descent. Actually, she loved *and* hated it. Loved that she'd reached her destination safe and sound, but hated knowing that this was the moment a tire could blow out and cause the plane to career off the runway.

Twenty minutes later, Myra found herself following the crowd and looking for someone in cleric attire who would be looking for her. She saw the young padre near the baggage carousel. He was holding a placard high in the air. Myra waved. She was rewarded with a wide, toothy smile as the cleric shouldered his way toward her.

"Mrs. Rutledge! I am Padre Tomás Diaz. Please, call me Tomás."

Myra held out her hand and smiled. "Only if you call me Myra. I just have one small bag. Thank you for meeting me on such short notice and at this hour of the evening."

They made small talk about her flight, the weather, the time change as they waited for Myra's bag to pop up out of the chute. Myra pointed to her beige plaid bag. The padre reached his long arm forward. Myra couldn't help but notice the frayed cuffs of his suit jacket.

"Follow me, Señ . . . Myra. I was fortunate in finding a parking space right in front." He smiled ruefully as he pointed to his collar. "It comes in handy sometimes. We have an hour's drive ahead of us. Unfortunately, Padre Mendoza will not be awake to welcome you. He retires early these days."

"Is he not well?"

"His health is fine, thanks to Countess de Silva. As Padre puts it, his old bones are deteriorating faster than his mind. My bishop sent me here to help out. That's another way of saying I do the heavy lifting. Padre Mendoza works with the children, teaching them their catechism and playing the organ while they sing. He spends a good part of each day sleeping if he is not praying in the chapel. He deserves the rest."

"I'm sorry to hear that. The countess has spoken of him more times than I can remember and always with love and respect." The young padre nodded as he settled Myra's bag in the back of his rusty pickup truck, which smelled like chicken poop.

"We have a truck like this at the farm," Myra said, and giggled. "Can we take just a moment? I want to call my husband to let him know I arrived safely." Myra looked down at her cell phone to see she had no bars. "Oh, dear, I forgot to charge the phone before I left. By any chance do you have a cell phone, Tomás?" She knew she could pull out the special phone she carried, the one that all the Sisters had, but something cautioned her not to do it.

"I do, but it won't help you. It is just for local use. Our cell phone use in the village is not what you are used to. Our cell towers are fitful at best.

"Now, about this truck. It runs, in case you are worried. It will get us to the parish house safe and sound. The countess ordered three new trucks for the village, but they have not arrived as yet. Customs, so much paperwork, and Padre Mendoza tends to ignore the mail. I believe the trucks arrived at the port, but when he didn't respond, they were sent somewhere else. We use the trucks to transport our pomegranates, figs, jujubes, and citrus fruits to the bigger cities. It's how the village survives, with the countess's help. God always provides, one way or another," he said happily.

"Fasten your seat belt. We're going to be traveling over some cart tracks. But I am a good driver, so you will be completely safe."

"I'm not worried, Padre Tomás. Tell me, when did you see the countess last? By the way, your English is very good." Myra asked her question as she looked around at the crowds of people. Did everyone travel at night? she wondered.

"Padre Mendoza told me when I arrived that the only thing the countess asked for in return for her help, and that was that all the children, everyone actually, learn English. She hired a teacher from Madrid to come here, and the teacher is still with us. I'm sorry the windows do not go up and down. We try not to drive if it is raining," he joked. "But to answer your question, I have never met the countess. I only know what Padre Mendoza saw fit to share with me, which is basically nothing. He guards his relationship with the countess very closely. You do know, do you not, that the countess provides for the entire village? She sends all the older children to the university. She provides for our elderly. We have a constable and a small jail that has never been used. We have a doctor, a real drugstore with a pharmacist, and two nurses who see to everyone's health and well-being. Everyone in the village, even the children, have a cell phone. We even have satellite TV. There is nothing our villagers would not do for our kind benefactor. The countess supports our church, the school, everything. I cannot wait to meet her one day."

Myra digested all that she was hearing before she asked, "Is the countess on the mountain? Do you know?"

"I do not know. Padre Mendoza told me I was not to talk of the Countess de Silva. He said that is his job. What I do know is he said he knows of you but has never met you in person. He said the countess considers you like a sister. Is this true? When you called, he did not seem surprised."

"Yes, it's true. We grew up together as children. I love her as a sister. I value and treasure our friendship. That's why I am here."

"Like I said, I look forward to meeting her at some point in time."

Myra nodded. The rest of the bumpy ride

was made in virtual silence. Myra didn't mind. She was tired, and her mind was racing as she ran scenario after scenario over and over in her mind. How could Annie be here and this young priest not know? What if she wasn't here? What if this was a wild-goose chase? There were so many what-ifs she couldn't get a handle on anything. All she could hope for was that tomorrow, Padre Mendoza would have some answers for her. She moved restlessly in the cracked leather seat, with the jutting springs digging into her thighs.

"It's just another mile or so, señora . . . I mean Myra."

Thank God, Myra thought. "Tell me, Padre Tomás, how does one get up the mountain these days?"

The young priest laughed. "Very carefully. Padre Mendoza told me when the countess left years ago that the road, such as it was, became overgrown. One either arrives on a helicopter or one hikes the mountain. Two of our village boys are the only ones who have ever gone up and actually returned. One needs to be a mountain goat. Luis Ramon is off at the university, so it is his brother Franko who knows the way. Franko has shown his brother Berto, who is just thirteen, the way up and down. Padre Mendoza sends them up three or four times a year to check on the monastery. He then reports to the countess by phone.

"Is it your intention to go up to the mountain, señora? If so, I must advise against it. You will probably need to go back to the Barcelona–El Prat Airport tomorrow and make arrangements to go by helicopter."

"I see," was all Myra could think of to say.

She occupied herself by taking in the scenery outside, or at least what she could see of it in the dark. They were just passing through a stone archway covered in clinging flowers. Beyond the archway was the small village, a cluster of stone buildings with wide arches and red roofs.

"We're here, señora," said Tomás, after pulling past the smaller buildings and stopping the truck in front of a much larger and more imposing structure. "As you can see, it is very quiet and dark. Electricity here is a luxury. We try to conserve and use a lot of candles. I have a very powerful flashlight, so just follow close behind me till we get indoors."

The inside of the rectory proved to be a surprise to Myra. While small, it was so clean she was stunned. The furniture looked to be home crafted and polished to a high sheen. The word *cozy* came to mind. As she followed the young priest up a pair of what looked like hand-hewn steps, she sniffed. Candles and the scent of lemon followed her. It was not an unpleasant scent.

The room was small—a single bed, a chest of drawers with a pitcher and basin for a quick wash. A bottle of water, the seal intact, sat next to a bottle of holy water. She looked around for any sign of a bathroom when she saw a folded towel and washcloth at the foot of the bed.

"It's in the hall," the young priest said, and smiled. "Is there anything I can fetch you before you retire?"

Myra whirled around. "This is your bedroom, isn't it?"

"Yes, but it is no problem. There is a comfortable palate on the first floor. I will be more than comfortable. Padre Mendoza rises early. We usually have breakfast at six o'clock. Eggs fresh from the henhouse, our homemade sausage, home-baked bread, and fruit from our own groves. Simple fare."

"It sounds delicious. Thank you for going to all this trouble. Truly, I appreciate it."

"If there is nothing else, I will retire myself. It's been a long day. The village bell will wake you at five o'clock. That will give you an hour to prepare for the day and to meet Padre Mendoza."

Myra wanted to tell the young priest she wasn't going to sleep a wink and would be more than ready at five o'clock, but she kept quiet. When the door closed, she leaned back on the bed, surprised at how comfortable it was. She closed her eyes and was instantly asleep, jet lag finally catching up with her.

When the village bell rang at five o'clock, Myra bolted awake, shocked and stunned at the sound. Even more stunned that she'd actually slept through the night. She swung her legs over the side of the bed. Should she head for the bathroom, or wait to see if the elder priest got first dibs? She strained to hear any sounds coming from the hall. All she could hear was silence. She debated for a few minutes before she grabbed the towel and washcloth, believing that because she was a guest, the elder and younger priests would allow her to go first.

But before she did that she had to decide what to do about her cell phone. She pulled it out of her bag. No bars. "This is not good," she muttered. She whipped out the encrypted phone and did her best to get a connection but was unsuccessful. She struggled to remember what Tomás had shared about cell phone usage. She remembered him saying calls could come in easier than outgoing calls for some reason. She recalled having no problem calling the padre when she was back at Pinewood. A chill ran down her spine when she realized she was virtually cut off from Charles and the Sisters. The chill she was experiencing seemed to grow colder. That had to be why Annie hadn't gotten in touch.

What to do? When Charles didn't hear from her, would he go into mission mode? She blessed herself, hoping that was the case. Then a thought struck her. The monastery was high on the mountain. Wasn't there something about the higher you were, the better the cell phone reception. If true, why hadn't Annie called? Because she's being held prisoner on her very own mountain, Myra told herself. The chill she was feeling deepened.

Myra sucked in a deep breath as she wrapped

her arms around her chest before she headed
out to the bathroom in the hall.

When she returned to her room, she marveled that she'd just taken the shortest shower
of her life due to the trickle of water that
dripped from the showerhead. She sighed when
she thought of the special rain forest showerhead back at Pinewood.

Myra looked at herself in the small mirror
over the dresser. She wasn't happy with her appearance but realized it didn't matter. She
gathered up her belongings and stuffed everything into her travel bag. She left the room,
certain she'd left it as she found it. In the
kitchen, she saw a middle-aged woman at the
stove. She smelled coffee and sausage. That's
when she realized how hungry she was.

"Welcome, señora. I am Olympia. I cook for
the padres. My daughter and I clean here and
help out when we can. We bake the bread, and
my daughter makes the candles that are used
throughout the village. We try to conserve the
electricity."

Myra nodded and held out her hand. "My
name is Myra. I am a friend of Countess de
Silva."

Olympia made the sign of the cross and
smiled from ear to ear. "Our benefactor, *sí*. Yes,
we love her. What can I prepare for you, señora?"

"Whatever you make for the padres will be
fine. Should we wait for them?" Myra asked as
she eyed the round, little lady wearing a pristine white apron.

"The padres never vary with their timing.

They take their seat at the table and say grace just as I finish their toast. You will see." She giggled, showing a mouthful of square white teeth that looked like Chicklets. Myra smiled, believing every word the little woman said.

The table was set, the dishes plain and heavy, the silverware shiny and just as heavy. The napkins were soft as silk and had been laundered hundreds of times. Myra wondered if there was a washing machine in the village. She asked. The cook nodded and pointed to a doorway at the end of the kitchen next to a fireplace that was big enough to roast a whole steer.

The air in the kitchen suddenly changed. Myra looked around to see Padre Tomás holding the door for the elder padre. He called out a cheerful good morning.

Myra moved quickly to assist Tomás as he guided the elder padre to his seat at the table. He removed the two canes and set them aside. He looked like a little gnome, Myra thought. She corrected the thought immediately to a beautiful little gnome. He was no more than four feet eight in height, and his weight was probably under ninety pounds. Snow-white tufts of hair stood up in patches over his head. His eyes, which had once been cornflower blue, were now milky white with untreated cataracts. He wore round eyeglasses perched low on his nose.

Padre Tomás made the introductions. Myra was careful not to squeeze the gnarled old hand that was red and swollen with arthritis. When he spoke in English, his voice was heavily accented. He thanked her for making the trip on such short notice. He waved his hands, then did his best to clasp them together so he could say grace. Everyone, even Olympia, bowed their head. The moment the last words were spoken was the moment Olympia set a platter of thick-sliced buttered toast on the table.

"We can talk after we finish our meal. Food and the preparation need to be enjoyed when it is prepared with loving hands. Our hens delivered these eggs this morning just for you, Señora Myra," the old priest cackled.

Myra laughed as she looked down at the three eggs on her plate. In her life she'd never seen such glorious yellow-orange yolks that just begged to be sopped up with the inch-thick bread toasted to perfection. Two slices of sausage ringed the eggs, alongside a pile of figs dusted with sugar. A Maggie or Kathryn breakfast. There was no way in the world she could eat even half of the food on her plate. She fought with herself not to pull out her cell phone to take a picture of her breakfast plate.

Thirty minutes later, Myra stared down at her empty plate and her empty coffee cup. Charles was never going to believe this. Never. She looked over at Olympia, and said, "Thank you for the most wonderful breakfast I've ever eaten."

Olympia beamed her pleasure. "That's what Countess de Silva said when I made breakfast for her." Myra nodded as she watched Padre Tomás help Padre Mendoza to his feet. "Follow us, señora. We will go to the office, where you and Padre Mendoza can talk. I will be outside waiting to take you back to the airport."

Myra did her best to contain herself. She itched to get things under way but had to respectfully wait for the old priest to settle himself behind his battered old desk.

The old priest leaned forward and started to talk. He spoke haltingly at first, but the more he spoke, the easier the words flowed. "I want you to know I broke my promise to your friend Anna, who is this village's benefactor. I asked God for a sign that it was all right for me to do as you asked when you called. I am sad to say I did not receive an answer to my plea, so I had to make an earthly decision.

"Several months ago, three young men came here to the village. They wanted to know how to get in touch with Anna. They said if I did not tell them, they would come back here with more men and destroy the village and kill all the women and children. At first I thought there was something wrong with my hearing, but, to my dismay, that was not the case at all. They said they were Armand de Silva's sons. They said their mother had just died and that's how they found out who their true father was. They said they wanted their inheritance, and the only way to get it was to meet Anna and have her turn it over to them."

Myra gasped in horror. "But . . . but . . . that can't be true. Annie would have told me. Was Armand married to someone else? Before he married Annie? She never told me. Oh, dear God! Did you believe them, Padre?"

"Dear lady, I did not know what to believe at the time. In all the years I've known Anna, she never once hinted or alluded to anything like that. I married her and Armand right here in this village church. They both swore to me this was their first marriage. I had no reason to doubt either of them. It is entirely possible the young count had a dalliance or two and had children born on the other side of the blanket. Young men sowing their oats, as the saying goes. I could not discount it, so I had to give credence to the possibility it could be true. That's why I called Anna. I am responsible for our village and all the lives here. I had no other choice. May God forgive me for breaking my promise to Anna and agreeing to help you when you called."

"But . . . but . . . DNA can prove if it is true."

"Even here in this small village I know as do our people what DNA is. What would we have to compare it to? Armand, Jonathan, and Elena are at the bottom of the ocean. Armand was the last surviving member of the de Silva family. Spanish law and the Spanish courts are not like your American justice system."

"There must be something we can do. Is Annie being held hostage on the mountain? Do you at least know that?"

"I don't know, señora. I met her at the airport and arranged for her to be helicoptered to the mountaintop. We talked at length at the airport. Right there, at the airport, she made me swear to Jesus Christ that I would do nothing until she got in touch with me. I asked her how long that would be, and her response was *as long as it takes.* I gave her my word. And I've broken my word." Tears trickled from the milky-white eyes, down the wrinkled cheeks. Myra wanted to cry herself, but she held her tears in check.

"But if she is being held hostage, that has to mean those men took away her phone. She would have no way to contact you, Padre. What made you decide to help me when I called?"

"It's been way too long. I have thought of nothing else during the past weeks. During that time, there have been many helicopter flights to the mountaintop. If they carried people or supplies, I do not know. The whole village is worried for Annie. Me most of all. I'm an old man who spends his days praying. I wanted to involve Tomás, but in the end, I did not. When you called, I thought I had found the answer."

"I know all about trust and how much Annie treasures loyalty, but, Padre, don't you think that going to the proper authorities might help? They could send in SWAT teams or whatever the Spanish police do in situations like this."

"I did think of calling someone at Interpol, but in the end I tried to do what Anna would have wanted me to do. I gave my word, my promise. Right or wrong, I have to live with my decision."

Myra's temper finally flared. "Annie could be dead for all you know! Oh, my God! I don't believe this. You should have done something, Padre. It's not like it was a confessional confession. You should have done something!" She cried as sobs caught in her throat.

"Tomás!" Myra bellowed at the top of her lungs. "I'm ready to go!" she bellowed again. She looked down at the gnome-like priest. "This is on you, Padre!" she screamed. "If . . . If anything happened to Annie, I'm coming after you, and I don't give a good rat's ass if you're a man of God or not." Even as she ranted, Myra knew she would regret her outburst and beg the padre's forgiveness, but right now she simply did not care. Right now, the only thing that mattered was finding Annie safe and sound.

Myra ran from the room and barreled past Padre Tomás, shouting for him to move his ass and not caring if she was being politically correct or not.

I'm coming, Annie. I'm coming.

Chapter 3

Myra climbed into the battered, old pickup truck. Her facial expression was one of red-hot anger and disbelief. "Do not talk to me, Padre. Let's make this trip in silence. I don't want to say something I'm going to regret later on."

"Very well, señora. Please, allow me to say one thing before we settle into silence. I know nothing about what is going on. I have my suspicions, but it is not my place to question Padre Mendoza. If there is any way for me to help you, I will. But until you tell me what is wrong, there is nothing I can do."

Myra's mind raced as fast as her heart was beating. She heard the words, heard the young priest's offer. What could he do? Nothing, she told herself. Her brain continued to race.

What finally came out of her mouth surprised her. "Where can I get some duct tape?"

Tomás laughed. "In the glove box in front of you. This truck consists of yards and yards of the magical tape. If you need it, please take it."

Myra had to bang on the glove box three times before it finally fell open. She saw small hand tools and a roll of duct tape. She reached for it and stuffed it into her bag.

Tomás risked a glance at his passenger out of the corner of his eye. He didn't like what he was seeing. "Señora, anger is not the answer to whatever it is you are seeking. I am a good listener if you want to talk. Please, I implore you to remember Padre Mendoza's age and his special relationship with your friend, Countess de Silva."

Myra's eyes narrowed to slits. She turned to the priest and said, "There is forgiveness, then there is *forgiveness*. He waited *THREE* months, and he'd still be waiting if I hadn't called and traveled here. Annie could be dead for all he knows. He did nothing. *Nothing!*" Myra screeched at the top of her lungs. "If that's your definition of a special relationship, I don't want any part of it. If he cared about Annie, he would have gotten in touch with the proper authorities and let them handle it. Instead, he did nothing. *NOTHING!*" Myra screeched again.

She wanted to cry so bad that she bit down on her lower lip, drawing blood. Finally, she blurted her last words of the trip. "And he's a man of God! By doing nothing, he put Annie's life in more danger. I am holding him personally responsible for her well-being, and I don't care if he's a priest or not."

"I wish I knew what you were talking about, señora, but I do not."

Myra shot the young priest a withering, scathing look that said it all. She closed her eyes and didn't open them again until the rusty truck came to a stop at the far end of the airport, where four different helicopters were lined up outside a hangar that bustled with activity.

"Come with me, señora. You must purchase a ticket and check your bag." Myra nodded.

I'm coming, Annie. I'm coming.

The minute Myra stepped through the door of the make-shift ticket office was when *mission mode* kicked in. She wished the Sisters were here with her, but she was on her own. Well, she was up to the challenge. She could feel her pulse rate ricochet off the charts. She took a deep breath and opened her billfold for her credit card. She was told it would be thirty minutes before she could board.

Myra withdrew some bills and stuffed them into Padre Tomás's hands. "Thank you for all your help. You can leave now, I'll be fine."

The priest held out his hand. Myra shook it. She attempted a smile but failed. "I can't apologize, Tomás."

"No apology is needed. I understand."

Myra turned and headed to the door with a picture of a lady on it. Inside, she gasped. It was a tiny room with barely enough space to turn around. And it was filthy dirty. She longed for a medical mask. Well, she wasn't here to use the facility; she was here to do something. She hung her shoulder bag on the nail on the door. She rummaged until she found the duct tape. She rummaged some more until she found the special encrypted phone she and the other Sisters carried at all times. Compliments of Avery Snowden.

Myra pulled up her shirt, trying to decide if she should tape the phone to her back or to her stomach. It took just a moment to opt for her stomach. Quickly, she ripped off strips of tape, attaching them to the special phone. She wiggled and squirmed as she struggled to wrap the tape all around her waist. She patted the tape in place, satisfied that there were no bulges to be seen with the naked eye. If she had to go through a pat down, she felt confident since importance would be concentrated on her back and legs, and not her stomach. And if she was wrong, she'd know soon enough.

Myra felt meaner than a one-eyed snake as she exited the filthy bathroom. She walked out into the early-morning sunshine to wait for her call to board.

I'm coming, Annie. I'm coming.

The pilot, his English heavily accented, smiled as he strapped Myra into one of the two passenger seats. She asked him if he had a cell phone that she could borrow to send a text to America. He shook his head and mumbled something about cell towers, airport interference. He threw his hands in the air and scowled. And that was the end of that.

More than ever, Myra realized how alone she was at that moment. Her heart and her gut told her Charles would do something the moment he realized she hadn't contacted him as promised. Enough time had gone by since her arrival to warn him that something was wrong on her end even with the six-hour time difference. She closed her eyes as she felt the whirlybird lift into the air.

Behind her closed eyelids, Myra envisioned the girls along with Charles and Fergus in the war room, formulating a plan. Would he have called in the boys? Probably. The first thing he would do would be to ask young Dennis if they could use his private plane, which Dennis would immediately agree to. Maggie and Ted would be clicking away on their computers, trying to figure out angles. Jack would ask if they were all locked and loaded.

Myra looked down at her watch. She took a deep breath and blew it out in a loud *swoosh* that went unheard over the noise of the helicopter. She had to believe that Charles would leave no stone unturned. Not even a pebble.

She took another deep breath when she realized the helicopter was descending. She leaned forward to see the helicopter landing pad and almost choked when she saw a circle of men waiting to greet her. She craned her neck farther, looking for a sign of Annie. She blinked, then blinked again. Annie was not among the welcoming party.

Myra took a page out of Kathryn's playbook and cursed freely. "Son of a bitch!"

Then she muttered under her breath, "I'm here, Annie. I'm here."

Myra waited in the open doorway for the pilot to exit the plane, so he could catch her as she hopped to the ground. She thanked him and nodded when he whispered in her ear, "Be careful, señora." He was back in the helicopter and lifting off before Myra could gather her wits about her. Suddenly, she wanted to call the pilot back, to get back into the helicopter, but the moment passed. She wasn't going anywhere.

The five men who greeted her looked like Wall Street bankers, which confused her. She had been expecting thugs, hooligans. She clamped her lips shut and waited. One young man stepped forward and relieved her of her combination purse and rucksack. Another picked up her small suitcase.

"Welcome, señora," one of the Wall Street banker types said in flawless English.

"Who are you? Where is Countess de Silva?" Myra asked, gratified that her voice was strong and forceful.

"Names are of little importance. But if you insist on a response, consider my compadres and me the countess's formal welcoming committee. The countess was not expecting you, but I'm told she always rises to the occasion. I would imagine she is in the outdoor solarium. And your name is?"

Myra's eyes narrowed to slits. "Like you said,

señor, names are of little importance. Think of me as a neighbor stopping by for coffee. I was in the neighborhood and thought I would drop down for a visit."

"Ah, yes, American humor. Amusing, no?"

Myra grimaced. She struggled to think of something Maggie would say. "Whatever floats your boat."

"Ah, another American witticism. Come. I will personally take you to the countess."

Myra decided she'd had enough. She clamped her mouth shut and trudged across the concrete and onto lush green grass to follow her welcoming committee to the living quarters of the old monastery. *I'm here, Annie. I'm here.*

Myra stopped short when the small parade stepped off the lush lawn and onto the marble wraparound walled porch for want of another word. "I know the way from here, señor. I've been here before. I can find my way." She hoped her tone came across as steely as she meant it to be.

Obviously, it didn't, because Mr. Wall Street prodded her arm. "Nonsense. The countess would never forgive me if I allowed you to intrude on her presence unannounced."

Kathryn's playbook came into play. "Cut the bullshit, Mr. Wall Street. We both know who and what you are. And don't think for a minute I missed those shoulder holsters you are all wearing under those expensively cut suit jackets. Now, where the hell is my friend?"

Mr. Wall Street's eyes narrowed, and his

mouth stretched into a thin, tight line. "You are very observant. You Americans are extremely vocal, unlike us Spanish. Breeding and refinement are our mainstays."

Another page in Kathryn's playbook turned over. "You're a thug in a thousand-dollar suit packing a gun. You kidnapped the countess, and you have me under guard. Yes sirree, that makes you refined and well-bred. In America, we'd call you a glorified asshole."

Mr. Wall Street stared at Myra, who did not flinch at what she was seeing in the man's eyes. She stood tall, but her insides were shaking like Jell-O. Kathryn would say stand up to them and *never* let them see you sweat. She felt like her underwear was drenched. "I'm not afraid of you!"

"Then, dear lady, that is your first mistake." He rapped sharply on a massive teakwood door. "Are you decent, Countess?" he called out. "I have someone here who wants to talk to you."

Myra strained to hear a response but could hear nothing. A feeling of déjà vu swept over her when her captor opened the door. Myra grew light-headed at what she was seeing, as time and her memory swept backward. She saw it all in a quick glance, Annie in a white robe, her hair in a coronet on top of her head, the television tuned to The Weather Channel. She stopped in her tracks to stare at her friend. Everything was the same except . . . except when she was here before, standing in this same spot, Annie's eyes had been glazed and out of focus. Not so now. Her eyes glittered with hatred. Myra felt her spirits soar as her captor waited to see what would happen.

Myra ran to Annie, her arms outstretched. Annie remained in place as she allowed herself to be embraced. "What the hell took you so long, Myra?" she hissed in her ear. Myra almost blacked out. She caught on immediately.

"Oh, my God, what have they done to you?"

"Why are you here, Myra?" Annie asked in a low, shaky voice.

"Well, it *is* your birthday, Annie. We've never missed sharing each other's birthdays. I came all this way to celebrate it with you. You could at least pretend you're glad to see me."

Annie turned to her captor. "Can we have some privacy, please?"

Without another word Myra and Annie's captor turned and closed the door behind him.

Myra started to babble and couldn't stop because she was trying to figure out what Annie's eyes were telling her. "When I was here the last time, we went for a walk. Let's do that now, Annie. If you're up to it. We had such a great time back then. I am so glad to see you. Happy birthday, my friend. I bought you a lovely gift but left it home for fear they wouldn't let me bring it on the plane. You are going to love it. What's going on, Annie? Who are those men?"

"Yes, a walk would be nice. I take a walk every day. Come along."

Myra gasped at how raspy Annie's voice sounded. Almost like she didn't talk much these days. Annie didn't speak again until they were far enough away from the monastery that they couldn't be overheard. She herded Myra to a stone bench at the foot of a fat, round tree that towered high into the sky.

"Well, damn, Myra, it took you long enough. I expected you weeks ago. Do you have any idea what I've been going through? Do you? In case you haven't figured it out, I'm being held a prisoner here. And now you are, too. Did they take your cell phone?"

"They took everything I brought with me, but Avery's phone is duct-taped around my waist. They didn't pat me down. I don't even know if it will work up here or not. And just for the record, Annie, whose fault is that? You left a note for Fergus. You wanted no interference. We all did just what you said to do, we left you alone."

"Yes, yes, but I thought after a week or ten days you'd ignore it all and come looking for me. I counted on you. I really did. Did you stop in the village?"

"I did, and I did not leave a lasting impression. If it's any consolation to you, those people abided by your instructions. You trained them too well. I just hope that Charles went into mission mode when I didn't text him on my arrival. I do not know if help is coming or not. Is there any way to get off this damn mountain other than by helicopter?"

"No, we're too old to try climbing down. Even I know that. We're stuck here."

"Who are these people? What do they want from you? The padre did tell me that they threatened to destroy the village. Is that what this is all about? You feel responsible for the village."

"Yes, but it's more complicated than that, Myra," Annie said wearily, her eyes filling with tears.

"Looks like we both have a lot of time on our hands, so why don't you tell me everything, right now. We've never kept secrets from each other, and this is not the time to start."

"Sometimes there are some secrets that are never meant to be shared, Myra."

"I'm a good listener, Annie. And you of all people know I am not judgmental. Talk to me," Myra pleaded.

"If I don't, will you push me off the mountain like you promised the last time you were here?"

"No, Annie. The reason is that I cannot imagine my life without you in it. It can't be that bad. Talking things out usually helps. It's cathartic to unload something you've been carrying around forever."

Annie wiped her eyes with the sleeve of the flowing white gown. After she took a deep breath, she stared off into space for what seemed like hours. Finally, she slowly began to speak, haltingly at first; then the words came faster and faster, like a runaway train going down the tracks.

"Armand and I were like Romeo and Juliet. At least that's how I thought of us. He was a count, a penniless one at that, but I didn't know that in the beginning. The only thing he had inherited was this monastery. And that was the sum total of what he owned. It's a place of sanctuary.

"I thought that was so very romantic. We were already married before he finally told me that he was flat broke. But you know what, Myra, I didn't care. I loved him, and I . . . well you know how much money I have. I was perfectly content to share with him. We were so happy." Here, she paused before saying, wistfully, "At least I thought we were.

"I turned over the shipping end of my business to him, and he turned it into what it is today. I can't fault him for that. To be sure, he was away a lot. On business. I never once thought he would be anything but faithful to me. I had stars in my eyes and, to mix metaphors, could not see the forest for the trees.

"I lived for the hours when he would return to me. Literally lived for them. The truth was that I had been a love-starved widow for more years than I care to remember.

"Eventually, I got pregnant with Elena. Armand was beside himself with happiness. He started staying home more, started to send others to do whatever it was he had done on his business trips.

"But when that happened, something happened to me. I wasn't that lovesick widow anymore. I was about to become a mother. I started looking at Armand differently, letting my mind go back over the years before I became pregnant, and, finally, I began to put two and two together. When I did, I confronted him, and he didn't deny his philandering during those long absences.

"Spanish men are very emotional. He wanted to clear his conscience, he said, and I had to listen to it all. Do I have to tell you that I was sick to the depths of my soul at his confessions?

"Mostly, I was angry at myself for being so stupid and gullible. After Elena was born, as soon as I was able to travel, I returned to Virginia, to our old homestead. That's when you and I resumed our friendship. Our daughters became best friends the way you and I were. We both loved the whole idea.

"From time to time, Armand would make an appearance to see Elena. And, of course, to check on our finances. I made sure when I returned that my assets remained mine and mine alone. In essence, Armand now worked for me, and he did not like that at all. Not one little bit.

"The purse strings were pulled tighter. My people, Connor in particular, put Armand's feet to the fire, and to keep him in the luxury to which he had become accustomed, he signed off on everything. He was nothing more than an employee, though one with way too many perks.

"The only thing I had to promise was that I would take Elena to Spain every summer or until she no longer wanted to visit her father. That is exactly how the agreement was worded. I kept up my end of the bargain, and Armand kept up his.

"The summer Elena turned nine, Armand

showed up with a baby in a basket. He said his sister had died giving birth to the baby boy he had named Jonathan. He asked me if I would stay in Spain for a year until he could make other arrangements for the boy with distant relatives. The baby was sickly and never really regained any kind of robust health, even though we took him to the best doctors in Barcelona.

"Armand never did find anyone willing to take Jonathan. I tried, God, Myra, I tried to love that child, but there was a disconnect somewhere in his brain. He would sit for hours and stare at the wall. He would scream and yell. He had to be spoon-fed. Every chance he got, he would try to do something to harm Elena. There were times he wouldn't speak for weeks on end. Finally, I was at my wits' end, and I told Armand that he had to get a nurse or a nanny for him. I flat out refused to care for him any longer the day he tried to set Elena on fire. I packed her up and returned to Virginia.

"Of course, I had to explain to my financial people about the high medical bills, the nanny's pay, and a host of other expenses. I guess I said something that put them on alert because they tried to track down Armand's sister. Seems he never had a sister, or any other siblings, for that matter. The boy was Armand's son by a *lady of the evening* was what came back in the final report.

"I took Elena back to Spain the following summer as I had promised to do. By then I had decided that I was going to file for divorce. I

told that to Armand, and he was not at all
happy. That was the day he took both Elena
and Jonathan out on the boat. Elena didn't
want to go. She cried. I made her go. I did,
Myra, God help me, I did. I told her we would
leave the very next day and go home to Virginia, where she would be with Barbara forever
as her friend. I told her we would never ever
come back here. My promise was the only way
she would go on the boat with Armand. I've re-
gretted that promise every minute of my life
since then. How could I have been so stupid? I
told myself Armand was her father, and that I
had promised him I would bring her to see him
every summer. I always honor my promises,
Myra.

"And that promise cost me my daughter's
life."

Myra threw her arms around Annie and
hugged her tightly. "Dear God, how could you
have kept that to yourself all these years? Oh,
Annie, I wish I had known. I don't know what I
could have done, but I would have done something to help you. I understand how you feel.
It never goes away. Never. We just learn how to
deal with the pain and go on."

"Now you know why I stayed on the mountain following the boating accident. Guilt, my
loss. Nothing mattered until the day you came
here to get me. I will be forever grateful to you.
Forever and a day, Myra."

"Okay, that's the back story," Myra said, her
voice husky with emotion. "What's this new
story? Who are these people?"

"Three of them claim to be Armand's sons. The one who speaks English so fluently seems to be the one in charge. The others don't speak any English at all. At least I have never heard them speak anything other than Spanish. They don't realize that I understand Spanish better than I speak it. I let them think I don't know what they're talking about. The other two appear to be their friends. They all have guns. They want their father's money. They say they are entitled to it."

"Okay, but I don't understand. Why now? Why all these years later? What brought this all about?"

Annie laughed, an ugly sound. "From what Enrico told me, he's the one who speaks fluent English, they didn't know about me until their mother passed away six months ago. Armand was always in their lives from the time they were born, but they were told he was an uncle. They grew up, Enrico said, in a fine house with servants, they were given good educations, all paid for by their doting uncle. He showed me a whole album of pictures from babyhood until the time of the boating accident. He did say that Armand traveled a lot and wasn't always with them.

"Everything they had, Myra, was paid for with my money. When I saw the pictures, I got so sick to my stomach that I threw up on the spot. He walked away but left the album to torture me. I fought with myself not to look at those pictures, but in the end, I did. As a punishment. There were dates and times written under the pictures. I was able to link the times to his extended absences. The three of them are avid soccer players. Enrico said that his father was very proud of all of them. They lacked for nothing except his name. They carried the name of their mother, Araceli.

"He pointed out to me that it means 'altar of heaven.' He said his mother was a saint. The pictures of her in the album confirmed that she was a very beautiful woman. She looked . . . ethereal. I paled in comparison." Annie swiped at her eyes. Myra hugged her tighter.

"What is it exactly that they want from you, Annie?"

Annie stared off into space for so long that Myra had to prod her gently for her to respond. "Oh, they don't want much. Just for me to legitimize them and turn over to them their father's fortune." She made an ugly sound in her throat. "Like that's going to happen."

"Let me make sure I understand this. You are their prisoner here at the monastery and will remain a prisoner until you give them what they want. Is that right?"

"Yes, and now you're their prisoner also."

"Did you explain the situation, how Armand was penniless. Did you tell them all the intricate details of your fortune and how it is protected?"

Annie made the ugly sound in her throat again. "Until I was blue in the face and hoarse from talking. They didn't want to hear any of that. Enrico went to Barcelona, where they live, and from there he got in touch with my key people. Though he never showed me the paperwork, he said that Connor had faxed him all the agreements and contracts we had with Armand. Enrico said they were obviously bogus, that he does not believe any of it. He called me a lying, cheating gringo. Do you believe that? And a slut and a whore, all the while calling his mother a saint. He believes I snared his father away from them with my money. That was a little hard for me to swallow, I have to admit."

"So, we're stuck here unless someone comes to rescue us. In the meantime, we are at their mercy."

"That sums it up, Myra."

"And yet they let you roam around."

"Where can I go, Myra? The mountain is too treacherous. I should have had the damn cable car redone, but I had no plans ever to return here, so I didn't see the point to spending all that money. Do you think I haven't thought about trying to go down? Don't get any ideas. With bones as brittle as they are at our age, we wouldn't have a prayer of making it down safely."

"Father Tomás said two of the boys climb up here several times a year. He said they're like mountain goats."

"Yes, Berto and Franko. Wonderful young boys. I've been hoping that the padre would break his promise and send them up, but no such luck. All we have going for us is the encrypted phone you have tied to your waist and Charles and the girls. That's it, Myra. I'm glad you're here, but you shouldn't have come."

"What do you think their plan B is? If they are half as smart as you seem to think they are, they have to know the paperwork your people sent really is legitimate. Do you think the smart one will threaten to kill us if your people don't come through?"

"Absolutely. My people will not buckle. You don't get to be where I am without putting all manner of safeguards in place. There is a whole ten-inch-thick special book drawn up by a team of a dozen lawyers about kidnapping and what will and will not be done. Even if they kill me, my estate goes to you and the girls and various charities. They still wouldn't get a dime. Enrico refuses to believe that."

Myra digested Annie's words. "Are they killers, Annie?"

A veil dropped over Annie's eyes. She went completely still. Myra waited, dreading her dearest friend's response.

"I think they are, Myra. Yes, I think they are."

Chapter 4

It wasn't the first time that Fergus and Charles pulled an all-nighter when they were in mission mode. Far from it. But this was the first time they'd spent an all-nighter staring at each other across the kitchen table without saying anything meaningful to each other.

Lady and her pups alternated between growling and whining, not understanding the silence. Lady led the parade to the kitchen door and waited. Fergus dutifully opened the door, and the dogs walked out. Fergus blinked. They always ran, hoping to find a stray squirrel they were allowed to chase but not to catch. Pure and simple, the dogs were picking up on his and Charles's stress, to go along with Myra's noticeable absence.

Things would change momentarily when the crew arrived in response to the text that

Charles sent out a little after midnight, which read: **Urgent. Meeting at 7. Don't be late.**

Fergus looked down at his watch, then at the clock on the Wolf range—6:55.

He felt his insides start to curdle. He tried and couldn't come up with a time when he dreaded a meeting more than this one. He risked a quick glance at Charles, who was looking haggard and weary. Just the way he looked when Annie had left him in the lurch months ago.

Charles pointed to the monitor over the kitchen door and said, "They're here! I don't know about you, Ferg, but right now I'd rather step on a rattler than go through what is coming our way." Fergus decided there was nothing to say to that particular statement, so he kept his mouth shut. He did check the big Bunn coffeemaker to be sure the pot had finished dripping. No matter what, coffee, for some reason, had to come first. He himself would pass. He was so coffee-outed he knew he couldn't swallow another mouthful. Nor did he want to. As it was, his nerves were twanging all over the place and the meeting had yet to get under way.

Within ten minutes, the parking area in the courtyard was full of cars as Lady and her pups yipped and yapped and howled as if to say, at last some action. Lady led the parade into the house. It was Harry who handed out the treats, then bedlam ensued.

Charles and Fergus suffered through five long minutes of snapping and snarling, cursing and hand waving before he called a halt with two sharp blasts of a whistle he kept in his pocket. "This is getting us nowhere. Follow me and try not to kill each other on the way to the war room. I mean it. I'm in no mood for this type of behavior," Charles barked over his shoulder.

The gang went silent, never having heard this particular tone coming from Charles before, a true indication that this meeting was beyond serious. Even Lady and her pups stopped chewing long enough to look up at their master to see what was going to come next.

"Guard, Lady," Charles said gently to the magnificent golden retriever. Lady knew what to do; she dropped to her haunches, then stretched out across the kitchen threshold, her pups alongside her.

The group was halfway down the moss-covered stone steps that would take them to the war room when Fergus realized that no one had asked for coffee. There could be no better indication how serious this meeting was.

The moment everyone was settled with the customary salute to Lady Justice, all hell broke loose. If he'd been a turtle, Charles would have retreated into his shell, never to be seen or heard from again. But he wasn't a turtle, he was a mere human, so he suffered through the onslaught of shrill, ugly, hateful questions and recriminations. The stiff upper British lip he was known for failed him. All he could do was wait it out, which he did in complete silence.

When there were no more ugly words, when all the questions were asked, he waited a full minute that to him seemed like an hour before he responded.

"Before you decide to burn me at the stake, there are a few things you need to know. I want you to listen to me very carefully. I did exactly what Myra asked me to do. I sent you all a text telling you I had just dropped Myra off at the airport. I ask each one of you to ask yourself the same question. What would you have done if Myra swore you to secrecy? I know all of you. You would have done exactly what she asked of you. Why should I be any different? I am her husband, after all. Myra told me, she didn't ask me, she told me to wait to notify you until I got back to Pinewood. Therein lies the difference. She did that for one simple reason. She did *not* want any of you trying to stop her from going to Spain to find Annie and bring her back home. I did what she asked. You cannot fault me for that, girls and boys.

"Now, having said that, I want you all to know I tried to persuade her, using every tool in my box, to stop her from making the trip. Her mind was made up. There is no doubt in my mind that she would have sicced Lady on me and knocked me silly with a fry pan in the bargain. That's how determined she was to leave.

"Myra and Annie, as you all know, have what you young people would call a very tight relationship. There is a bond there that can never be broken. While they may not be related by blood, they are still closer than two blood sisters. I think you all know that.

"I think Myra *thinks* she knows something, but she did not choose to share that knowledge with me. Don't think I didn't try to get her to tell me, because I did. I also know when to back off and let Myra take the lead, which is precisely what she did. She said she would call when she landed. I believed her for the simple reason that Myra has never ever lied to me. That call never came. There could be any number of reasons why she never called. One, she forgot to charge the phone the night before. Two, there was no cell phone reception at the airport when she landed. Three, she had to find a place to charge her phone and was unable to do so. Four is unknown.

"Five is what *is* known, which is that it is almost twenty-four hours later, and there has still been no word from Myra. By now, she should have charged her phone if that was the problem, and if that didn't work, buy a new one and charge it enough to make at least one call. She did not do that for reasons we do not yet know. If you want my opinion, I think Myra is in trouble, as is Annie. The only consolation to me at this point in time is hoping they are together. Why else do you all think I called this meeting?"

"What you're saying is we need to get our ducks in a row and head for Spain as in immediately. Is that what you're saying, Charles?" Nikki asked.

"That's what I'm saying, yes."

"Myra has a twenty-four-hour head start on us. More like forty-eight hours until we can get this show on the road," Isabelle said.

"A lot can happen in forty-eight hours," Yoko said. "Add another twenty-four hours to that till we come up with a plan that is workable, and we're looking at seventy-two hours, possibly longer. This is not good. Not good at all."

"So we're going to Spain," Kathryn said, more of a statement than a question. "We're actually going to go back to that damn mountain where we lived for over a year before we got caught and had to take it on the lam. Damn. How are we going to get there?"

All eyes turned to Dennis.

"Is your plane available to us?" Jack asked.

"Absolutely, but the pilot is not," Dennis answered. "He just had hip surgery and is in rehab for another three weeks. He sends me updates in case I need the use of the plane. I'm sure he can recommend another pilot. The hostess is good; it will just take one call to put her on notice."

"Do it," Charles said, authority ringing in his voice. He heard the collective sigh from the group, which meant they were back on track.

"Where, exactly, are we going?" Maggie asked because she hadn't taken it on the lam with the others.

"Barcelona," Fergus shot back.

"And from there to the village? Do we have to climb the mountain? I remember very clearly the day Annie got a call from someone, probably the padre, but I'm not certain, and it really doesn't matter who made the call. We were having lunch outside on the terrace right here at Pinewood. Annie told us that the killer storm that hit Spain and was in the news, like, forever and had lasted for days had destroyed the cable car and part of the mountain. She said it would cost millions to build a new one, and since we were never going back there, she didn't see any point to having it rebuilt. I also remember how we were all deathly afraid to even step foot in it. Depending on one's stamina, it takes two, three, or four days to hike up to the mountaintop if I recall correctly. Or is there a better way to get there all these years later? Once I left there, I cast all those memories aside, never to be revisited."

"How certain are you that is where Myra went?" Kathryn said. "I can't even remember the name of the village. Do any of you remember it?" No one had a memory of it.

Fergus and Charles looked like two deer caught in the headlights.

"As certain as we can be at this point in time. To my knowledge, Myra does not know anyone in Spain. No one at all," Charles repeated emphatically.

"Annie just called the village 'the village.' She never to my recollection called it by a name. She spoke of the padre. His name was Santos Mendoza. He's quite elderly. She didn't talk about it all that much to me. Bad memories and all that," Fergus said.

"Neither Myra nor Annie ever mentioned the

name to me, either. For all I know, it doesn't
have a name. I never saw any maps. Fergus is
right about the priest's name, though. I do
know that at some point a helicopter pad on
the mountain was created. Something about
erosion on the mountain itself. I think I remember Annie's saying it was too treacherous
to climb. But my memory is telling me I heard
that years ago," Charles said, "after all of us
left. Kathryn is right about the cable car. Annie
called it a death trap. I think we all agreed with
her."

"What's the name of the monastery?" Maggie asked. "I can Google it, and maybe we can
find out the name of the village that way."

"I don't know if it has a name. Annie just re-
ferred to it as the monastery. Since it was in the
de Silva family, see if you can go by that," Fergus said.

"I never heard either Myra or Annie refer to
it by a name," Charles said.

"In other words, we're going to Spain blind,
with no clue as to our destination," Ted said,
tongue in cheek. "I realize all the girls know
the place because they lived there, but to the
rest of us, this is all Greek. We need to do better than that."

"Myra called the priest. I do know that because she said so. So she had a phone number
to call," Charles said. "And, no, I don't know
where she got the number, so it won't do you
any good to ask me."

"Did she call on her cell or a landline?" Espinosa asked.

"When she told me, she waved her cell phone under my nose, so I think it's safe to assume she used her cell, and, of course, she has that with her, so there is no way to find the number unless Annie left her address book behind. Did she, Fergus?" Charles said.

"No, that was the first thing I looked for after she left. Either she took it or she hid it, but that makes no sense. Yet in a way it does make sense if she didn't want us to know what she was up to. I think she took it with her if my opinion counts. She always kept it on a shelf above the little workstation she has for paying bills and such in the kitchen, where her laptop was. It was gone when I looked."

"People, does Montserrat, Spain, ring a bell?" Maggie said, looking up from her laptop.

The gang shook their heads.

"Why?" Nikki asked.

"Because there is a huge monastery there, high in the mountains. It's a Benedictine retreat for monks. It says it offers spectacular views of Catalonia. There is a holy grotto there where it is said the Virgin Mary visited. According to what I am reading, it is one hour northwest of Barcelona by train. Probably shorter if you flew by helicopter. It's all I'm finding right now. Does any of that ring a bell?" Charles and Fergus shook their heads. Maggie shrugged and went back to tapping on her laptop.

"Isn't Montserrat a tourist attraction?" Alexis asked. "I think I read something in the Sunday travel section once awhile back. Our time on the mountain is a bit of a blur these days. It seems like it was all a hundred years ago."

"Yes, it is," Maggie mumbled.

"Maybe there is more than one monastery. Aren't there many more mountains? Annie's monastery was family owned by Annie's husband. Off the beaten track is what I recall. Very private, that's why we hid out there. We kept the cable car on the platform so no one from down below could take it willy-nilly. The people in the village and the padre were our warning system." Alexis clarified, "They used bells that could be heard all the way up the mountain. One peal was for one thing, two for something else. Three was Red Alert. I remember that." The others nodded in agreement.

"I'm checking," Maggie mumbled.

"Maybe we're going about this all wrong. Maybe we should concentrate on the priest, or padre as they call priests in Spain. Padre Mendoza has to belong to some order. Benedictine? Franciscan? What? We should try to find out who his bishop is. Maybe that will help us," Dennis said.

"Good thinking, kid. Have at it," Ted said. Dennis blushed as he started tapping at his keyboard.

Jack looked at Charles and voiced a question. "Should we alert Avery Snowden? He has sources that are unavailable to the rest of us. I think we should if my vote counts."

Charles didn't bother asking for a vote. He simply nodded and sent off a text to the old spy.

Dennis held up his hand, an indication he needed to be heard. Dennis was always polite. Sometimes to a fault. Charles nodded, and the others stopped talking and waited. "My pilot called a colleague, and he agreed to make the trip. He's good for as long as we need him. He is right now on his way to the airport to get the plane ready. He will advise when we're good to go. Ditto for the hostess. I think her name is Beverly Adams. We've used her before. No more than three hours tops."

"Great! All set to go with no destination in mind," Harry grumbled. "This sounds like one of Jack's harebrained plans."

"Not true, Harry, not true. We know we're going to Barcelona. What we don't know is where we're going once we get there. To which village, to be precise. This pilot can get us to Barcelona. Chew on that, Mr. Smartass," Dennis said through clenched teeth.

Eyes popped, jaws dropped. Did politically correct Dennis West, intrepid reporter, just call Harry Wong a smartass? Eyes grew wider as they all stared at Harry, then Dennis.

"You're on the ball, kid. I like that. I stand corrected," Harry said, grinning from ear to ear.

"What the hell, Harry, are you sick or something? You running a fever? Any other time, you would have laid the kid out cold," Jack hissed in Harry's ear.

"I misspoke, Jack. It's that simple."

"Get away from me. You might be contagious," Jack stage-whispered. Harry laughed.

Jack could count on both hands how many times he'd actually heard Harry laugh. Especially out loud. Like maybe twice. Jack shivered. Under the table, Cyrus whined.

Dennis looked like he wished the floor would open up and swallow him whole. He couldn't believe he'd just spoken to Harry the way he had. He was about to apologize when Harry winked at him. The reporter deflated like a pinpricked balloon.

"Avery is on board," Charles said, reading an incoming text. "He said he can be wheels up in two hours. He'll be in touch when he lands in Barcelona. He said the first thing he will do is check in with Centro Nacional de Inteligencia, which is the equivalent of the CIA and MI6. He said he has some longtime sources he can tap for good intel. His first order of business will be to get as much background on Annie's husband, Count Armand de Silva, as he can. He said starting at the bottom and the very beginning always works best and saves time and trouble in the end."

Kathryn let loose with a snort of disgust. "Is he aware of the count's death so many years ago? If so, I think that's a waste of time. We simply do not have time to pussyfoot around. Time is of the essence. We're dealing with real time here. The here and now." She looked around at the others to see what they felt. One by one, they shrugged as much as to say, you know Avery, he does it his way, and he always comes through in the end. Kathryn threw her hands in the air.

And that was the end of that.

Charles fished around for the whistle in his pocket. He gave it two sharp blasts. "Listen up. With time of the essence, as Kathryn just so aptly reminded us all, I suggest we disperse. Go home and do what you all have to do. We'll all meet up at the airport in three hours, four if needed. Dennis will apprise the pilot when we're ready to go. I've got to locate our dog-sitter and get things set up here. I know you all have things you need to do."

"What about Cyrus?" Jack asked.

Charles looked at the steely glint in Jack's eyes and nodded. "He can come. We'll make it work. Make sure you all have your passports, and unplug all your appliances since we don't know how long we'll be gone. Kathryn, notify Jack Sparrow as to our plans. Abner, you're staying behind, is that right?"

"Yes, that's right. I still can't fly because of my ears. I can stay here at the farm and take care of the dogs if you like."

"Deal!" Charles shouted happily. "One less thing for me to worry about. And, people, while you're preparing for the trip, try to recall as much as you can about your time on the mountain. Even if it seems unimportant, it still might be useful to us."

Isabelle planted a lip-lock on her husband that turned Charles's face pink. Abner looked dazed when he watched his wife scamper after the others.

* * *

The group was solemn and silent as they climbed the portable stairway to the interior of the luxurious Gulfstream. Not so Cyrus, who barked happily and raced up the steps and into the passenger area, where he waited for his master. He knew what a plane was, and he loved to fly. Because . . . whenever the plane landed, there was always *action*. He loved sitting like a person and being buckled into his seat. Loved that everyone paid attention to him with ear scratches and belly rubs and more than his share of treats. He did his best to nudge everyone along, so he could settle in. He looked up at Jack to see where his treasures were—his security blanket and Goldy the duck, which was nothing more than a lump of worn-out material these days but still his most treasured possession.

The minute the Gulfstream reached its cruising altitude, and everyone was settled in for the six-hour plane ride, Maggie zeroed in on the girls, and said, "Tell me what it was like living on that mountain for all that time. I want to hear everything. How can you not remember the name of it? That's just too weird."

"It was a boot camp, pure and simple. Charles was the worst drill sergeant ever born. When we weren't training, and I'm talking combat training, we were in a classroom learning languages," Isabelle said.

"At the end of the day, we were too tired to eat our evening meal, and the food was out of this world. All we wanted to do was sleep. We were in tip-top shape at the end of the year.

And we were so in demand by other countries that we had to turn down most of them. That's how we became so notorious. And the best part of all that was we could name our own price. I don't even want to think about how many missions we did while we were there, but that's the main reason our coffers are so robust," Nikki said.

"I'm speaking for myself here, but I dread going back there. Too many memories. Not all of them good, either. I think it's true what they say when they say that you always want the one thing you can't have. For me, that was to come home and drive my truck again. I had to make the best of it, and I did. Truly, I dread setting foot on the mountain," Kathryn said.

Maggie's head bobbed back and forth as she watched the Sisters nodding, agreeing with everything that Kathryn and Nikki had said.

"The place was like a fortress. A prison, if you will. It took a lot of getting used to, I can tell you that," Yoko said. "We all learned six different languages. None of us were fluent in any of them, but we all learned enough to survive in a country, say Germany, which is a hard language to begin with. I don't think I remember any of them at this point in time."

"In the end, though, we all excelled to the point we were better than the guys Charles brought in to train us. In fact, two days after the last test and trial, we went up against the instructors, and we aced it. Those instructors were hard-core, and we beat them," Nikki said proudly.

"Charles couldn't believe it. Those guys left the mountain with their tails between their legs," Kathryn said. "You know what, I don't want to talk about this anymore. The 'past is prologue,' as they say." The others agreed. Maggie sighed and went back to her laptop.

In the front of the plane, the guys were clustered together. "This might be a good time for you to clue us in on things, Charles. I think I can speak for the others that none of us know anything about that period of time when we were not included in what was going on. Nikki never talks about it. We all had *stuff* going on during that time. I get all that. But now we need to know. If the girls won't talk about it, that leaves you, Charles. You were there.

"Fergus and the rest of us weren't. What are we walking into? What the hell could Annie be involved in that was so important that she sidelined all of us? That's simply not the Annie we all know and love. Spit it out, Charles."

Charles spoke for almost an hour, explaining how they'd gotten to the mountain, their lives there up until they had to relocate. He wound down, saying, "I have no earthly clue what would make Annie pick up and leave like she did. She has no family except for all of us, so that isn't even a consideration. If something happened to the monastery, she wouldn't much care. She said it was a financial drain and didn't care about it. She did care about the village and the people, especially the padre. I doubt it's the village. Sad to say, I am as much in the dark as the rest of you."

All conversation ceased when the hostess named Beverly, a willowy blonde with a perpetual smile, appeared with a service cart full of drinks and a large tray of canapés. "I hope this is all right; I didn't have all that much time to be too selective. I had to make do with what the caterer could put together on such short notice. We won't run out, that's a given, so eat hearty, gentlemen."

The gang settled for coffee and the pretty little sandwiches, which were no more than a bite each. The consensus was they were tasty and the coffee delicious. Within minutes, the tray was completely empty. The hostess replenished it immediately before she moved to the back of the plane to serve the women.

By the time the plane landed, the entire group was wired to the nth degree—even Cyrus, who was tired of eating the strange food he had been given.

On landing, Jack was the first off the plane, with Cyrus, so he could find a place to do his business. They returned just as a large black Chevy Suburban pulled alongside the plane.

Next stop, Customs.

Chapter 5

Desperation rang in Myra's voice. "We need a plan, Annie. Think. There must be something we can do. Some way to outwit them. We aren't stupid. There has to be a way, we just aren't seeing it.

"Let's start with the fact that they need you alive, so that rules out their killing us, at least for now. What I'm not getting is that these guys are so patient. Too patient. I can tell you that if it comes to that, I will go down fighting. Charles . . . Charles and the girls will find a way to get here. I know it. I feel it. Now, goddamn it, Annie, think."

"Ah, I see we're going by Kathryn's playbook and cussing. Okay, that works for me. What the hell do you think I've been doing all this time besides thinking. We're stuck here. Our options seem to be: one, getting gunned down; two, pushed off the mountain; or three, killing ourselves trying to go down the mountain.

"None of those three options are looking very appealing to me at the moment. You want to take a shot going down the mountain, go for it, but count me out. I can't decide if these guys are killers or not. I know they threatened to kill the padre and the villagers, but that might just have been a threat. The two brothers appear, at least to me, to be different from Enrico. He's the one who is obsessed with all this; the other two are just going along with him for reasons that are known only to them. I do not think that they even like him.

"Spanish people tend to be very religious, and killing is a sin. I do think you're right, though, we're safe, at least for now. They need me.

"Your best guess, Myra, how long before Charles and the girls can get here?"

"Three days, four. That's a guess. Do you really think we're safe for that period of time?"

"I wish I knew, Myra, but I simply do not know. I think they're trying to wear me down. We have to find a way for you to use that phone. We're being watched right now even though we can't see anyone. They're suspicious now with your unexpected arrival. They are viewing you as a wild card. They were not expecting you, and they're trying to figure out what your visit means. I'm thinking they are going to fall back and regroup, and that can't be good for either one of us. By now, they have certainly gone through your luggage and your backpack. And, hopefully, they have found nothing other than your regular cell phone, which you said is dead."

"Did you ever stash a gun here anywhere?"

Annie shook her head. "The answer is no. They took the one I brought with me. When I first got here, I wandered all over the place, checking out all the buildings from when we trained here. There wasn't so much as a paper clip left behind. They had removed all the knives that were in the kitchen, too. I was hoping for at least a small paring knife I could shove in my pocket or up my sleeve, but no such luck."

"What do you think their end game is, Annie? Do you see it as their intention to keep you here and wear you down or . . . or what? They have to be feeling the stress. How long are *they* prepared to hold out? What's *their* breaking point?"

"The brothers have been arguing among themselves this past week. In Spanish. Flavio, the youngest, wants to leave. He's worried about his fiancée. Enrico slaps him down several times a day. Mateo is getting antsy. I think he's a womanizer and wants to go back to having a life. He's been getting mouthy the past few days. The other two are just flunkies, goons, if you will. They do what they're told, nothing more, and for the most part don't even talk; at least I haven't heard them.

"Before you got here, the three brothers

were talking. Enrico said they should stop coddling me and show they mean business. What he meant specifically was to pull out my toenails, my fingernails, then my teeth. He seemed to think that would convince me to tell my people to pay up."

"Oh, my God!" Myra gasped.

"Mateo told him to shut up. Those were his exact words, *shut up*. He said they were not barbarians. That's why I think it was just a threat about the padre and the villagers. Then they all had a big fight. I don't think they resolved anything. And then suddenly you showed up. That threw them for a loop, I can tell you that. They didn't know what to do.

"They were prepared to shoot whoever got off that helicopter. I don't think to kill, just shoot to wound, to incapacitate. I guess that shooting someone is not quite the same as torturing someone in their eyes. To them, shooting someone is simply taking care of business."

"If Charles and the gang get here, they will outnumber the five of them."

"Myra, look at me. They have automatic weapons. Later, or tomorrow, we can take a walk out to the old shooting range where Charles had us all practice so I can show you what they've done to it. It's nothing but splinters. I don't know if all their practice shooting was for their own amusement or if they're planning on starting a war, but they're excellent shots. Even if I had my gun, which they took when I got here, I could never take them out.

Maybe one or two if the shots were perfect, but
that still leaves the other three. We're stuck,
pure and simple."

"Well, I'm not giving up," Myra said. "Where
there's a will, there's a way."

"Come on, it's time to go back. They don't
let me roam for more than an hour at a time.
I've got bruises all over my back and arms from
the goons who prodded me with their rifle
butts if I didn't move fast enough to suit them.
I found it best to do just as I'm told. If I argued
or put up a fight, they withheld food and
shower privileges. Just so you know, Myra."

"So we toe the line until help gets here, is
that what you're saying?"

"As much as I hate to admit it, yes, that's
what you have to do. Ah, I was right, our hour
is up, and here comes Mateo. Don't even look
at him."

"Only one of them looks like Armand. I
guess the other two look like the mother."

"Yes, he does. Enrico even has his father's
mannerisms. This whole thing is just eating at
my soul, Myra. How could I have been so in-
credibly stupid?"

"Cut yourself some slack, Annie. It's not like
back then you were worldly and sophisticated.
You were in love with a handsome, dashing
count. Whatever or whoever came before you
wouldn't have mattered. You lived in the moment and were happy. Stop beating yourself
up. None of us can un-ring the bell."

"So now you're my voice of reason, is that it?"

Myra grimaced. "Far from it. This might be

a good time for me to tell you I never liked Armand. I thought you were too good for him. I thought he was a gigolo. I never said anything because you were so happy. You wouldn't have listened to me back then even if I had voiced my opinion."

"You're right, I wouldn't have listened. And here we are."

"Yes, here we are. At least we're together. That has to count for something," Myra said.

A shadow crossed their path as Enrico Araceli appeared out of nowhere. He motioned for the women to follow him. They did so because they had no other choice.

The Spaniard led them up a flagstone path that led to an outdoor pavilion furnished with decrepit-looking wicker furniture. The television on the one solid wall was tuned to The Weather Channel, but it was set to mute. Myra blinked as she remembered the first time she had set foot on the mountain. He motioned for them to sit. They did.

While they were gone, Enrico had changed his clothes. He now wore khaki cargo pants, Timberland boots, and a pristine white polo T-shirt. It showed off his bronzed skin, his electric-blue eyes, and his glistening white teeth. Maggie would say he was ripped. Meaning he was muscular and in good shape. The shoulder holster complete with gun added to his physical badass presence. He could have been a Ralph Lauren model minus the firepower.

Enrico wasted no time. "Why are you here, señora? Who sent you? Do not lie to me."

Myra tried to settle herself more comfortably on the wicker chair. She hoped she was giving off an air of nonchalance. "I told you on my arrival that I came here to celebrate the countess's birthday. All our lives, we've celebrated our birthdays together. No one sent me, señor. I came here on my own. Just for the record, I've been here before, many many years ago."

"How did you know the countess was here?"

"What kind of silly question is that? She told me where she was going when she left Virginia. She said if she wasn't back for her birthday, I would have to come here. And as you can see, here I am. What is going on? Am I being held as a prisoner? Where are my things? I always heard and thought that the Spanish were excellent hosts. What do you hope to gain by keeping me here, if that is your plan?"

"I ask the questions, not the other way around. I don't believe a word you said.

"Now, who sent you? Who else is coming here?"

"I think you just called me a liar, señor. I am not a liar, and I resent the implication that I am. I told you, no one sent me. Who else would be coming? I don't know anyone in Spain," Myra huffed indignantly.

"Do you think I'm a fool, señora?" Enrico snarled.

"I don't know if you are a fool or not, but what I do know is you are certainly acting like a fool right now," Myra said brazenly. She tried not to flinch when Annie pinched her thigh for her to tone down her words. She ignored what she knew later would be a delicious purple bruise and held the Spaniard's gaze. She felt elated when the Spaniard looked away first.

"I know that you are lying to me. I expect within hours there will be people dropping from the sky and climbing the mountain. It won't matter; we'll be gone by then. Our ride, as you Americans like to say, will be here shortly."

"Where are we going?" Annie asked hesitantly.

Myra's shoulders sagged. She hated the defeated look on Annie's face but knew she wore the same look. If Enrico spirited them away, Charles would never find them. She'd come so far, and now, when the rescue team arrived, there would be no one at home to rescue. She wanted to scream, but the tears she saw in Annie's eyes made her stifle the sound building up in her throat. "You're not going to get away with this. We're Americans. Our people will come looking for us. Sooner or later, you will be tracked down and held accountable." How brave that all sounded, Myra thought, and how impossible.

"Yes, señora, I am. This is my country. My rules. My laws. You would do well to remember that. You also need to remember that my brothers are not as kind as I am. Now, no more talking. You each have ten minutes to use the bathroom; then our ride will be here. You will bring nothing with you. Is that understood?"

Annie nodded, so Myra did as well.

Ten minutes to get ready. Two to pee and eight to unwrap the phone and try to make a call. But would there be reception in a bathroom? Myra had no way of knowing.

Myra looked over at Annie, and she could see she was thinking the same thing she was thinking. "You go first, Myra, I can wait. Don't worry, the bathroom is the one place these . . . these gentlemen don't spy on you. There's nothing in there but soap and a dirty towel. There's not even a damn window," Annie said, her eyes burning feverishly.

Myra moved faster than she had ever moved in her life. She had the encrypted phone ripped off her stomach in a nanosecond. She powered it up, holding her breath to see if she could see the bars that ran across the top of the special phone. There was a battery, but it was weak and flickering. She flexed her fingers, which were shaking badly. She punched in the numbers and waited. *Pick up, Charles. Pick up, Charles. Please, God, let him pick up.* When she heard her husband's voice she almost fainted. She skipped the amenities and blurted, "There are five of them, we're being held hostage here at the monastery. They are Armand's children; they want Annie's money. Hurry, Charles, they're moving us off the mountain. Are you there, did you hear me? Oh, God, Charles can you hear me?" She listened, holding the phone so hard against her ear her head started to pound. She knew Charles was talking, but she didn't know what he was saying. And then the phone died.

Myra wasted no time trying to power up again, knowing it would be fruitless, and she was under the gun time-wise. She quickly strapped the phone around her waist again, peed, then flushed. She ran her hands under the cold water but didn't dry them on the dirty towel. She exited the small room to allow Annie to enter. She started to pace, to Enrico's amusement. She ignored him, her eyes blazing with hatred.

Annie joined her just as the *whump whump* sound of a helicopter coming in to land on the pad shattered the air.

"Move, ladies."

Enrico was so close behind her that Myra could have reached back with her foot and kicked him. She resisted the urge when she heard Annie hiss, *"Break your pearls."*

Myra blinked, not sure she had heard her friend correctly. Then she understood immediately. Since they didn't have any bread crumbs, her beloved heirloom pearls would have to do. She closed her eyes and yanked at the pearls.

Enrico reached out and grabbed each of them by the arm, his grip fierce and tight as the helicopter powered down, the rotors screaming in the early-evening darkness as the air around them kicked up and almost lifted them off the ground, hence the tight hold on their arms.

"Damn you, look what you made me do?"

Myra screeched at the top of her lungs. It sounded like a whisper over the roar of the helicopter's engine. "Those were my great-grandmother's pearls! Wait! Wait! I have to gather them up. Annie, help me. Please!" Tears rolled down Myra's cheeks as she jerked free of Enrico's tight hold to try to gather up the scattered pearls.

Myra suddenly found herself jerked upright when Enrico pulled her up by the collar of her shirt. His other arm reached out to Annie. "On your feet. Forget the beads." Myra cried hysterically, hoping she was pulling it off.

Enrico made sure the two women were securely buckled into the wobbly seats that had been patched and repatched a hundred times with yards and yards of duct tape. Then he said something to the pilot, who nodded in response. Myra looked past Enrico and saw the two brothers and the two goons watching and waiting for the helicopter to lift off. Another whirlybird must be on the way to pick them up, she thought. She looked around to see where Enrico was to sit, but there were no other seats, so he would hold on to the overhead bar by the open door. She hoped the pilot would encounter turbulence and Enrico would fall out.

The high-pitched whine of the turbo blades hurt Myra's ears. She clamped her hands over her ears when she saw Annie cover her ears. Enrico did nothing as the bird lifted, then made a right turn and headed out for parts unknown. Myra's stomach was one big knot of pain.

Annie inched closer to Myra. For all intents and purposes, they were little girls again at their first dance recital, when they were frightened out of their minds because they would have to take to the dance floor and perform for an audience.

Myra had cried that day. She remembered how she'd squeezed up to Myra so tight that they had to be pried apart. Annie reached for Myra's hand and clasped it between her own hands. She hoped the gesture comforted Myra as much as it comforted her.

Ninety minutes later, when the helicopter started to descend, Myra had to accept the fact that with no turbulence, Enrico Araceli was still alive and well, and not splattered on the rough terrain below. She couldn't help but wonder if she would ever be able to hear normally again.

After leaving the helicopter, Myra looked around as she juked under the blades, which were beginning to slow down. Enrico had hold of one of her arms, while he had hold of Annie with his other hand. Clearly, he was taking no chances that they would bolt. Everything looked the same, just the time of day was different. It was now dusk, with dark purple shadows everywhere beyond the hangar and the bright lights on the runway and inside the hangar. She didn't see anyone she could call to for help. She struggled to remember what she could about the layout. Where could she run? Would he chase her? Not if he wanted to remain in control of Annie. He'd have to let her go. Where was his gun? Probably in the back of his cargo pants, with the polo shirt covering it. Could she do it? Could she make a run for it? Did she have the stamina? Where would she go? She had no money. All she had was the encrypted phone around her waist. And she didn't even know if it could be powered up again or not.

Myra craned her neck to see past the bright lights, and heard a car engine even before she saw the vehicle. Their ride. Like hell!

Without any warning, Myra jerked free and started to scream at the top of her lungs, "Let me go, you damn pervert! Take your filthy hands off me!" She ran then, like all the bats in hell were after her, across the tarmac to the access road, then to the concrete path that led to the main terminal, all the while screaming, "He's a pervert, a molester, and he has a *GUN!*"

Myra continued with her wild run, which had started at sixty miles an hour. She was barely hobbling now, with stomach spasms and leg cramps so intense she could barely catch her breath. She prayed, childhood prayers she said every day of her life, as she clutched at the door that would lead her into the terminal. She was aware of the curious looks she was getting, but no one stopped her, no one seemed to think she was in peril. God in heaven, why was that? She looked around wildly for a restroom. She spotted the sign directly ahead. She didn't look back, she was too afraid. She had to get to safety, where there were people. Women in particular, who would help her. She had to see if the phone worked.

Myra slammed against the restroom door and gasped when she fell into the lightest, brightest room she'd ever seen in her life. She was shaking from head to toe and could barely breathe she was so light-headed. She collapsed onto a leather bench next to what she thought was an infant's changing table. She continued to struggle to breathe, stomach spasms making her double over. Her leg cramps made her want to scream, and she would have, at the top of her lungs, but she had to concentrate on her breathing. All she could do was endure and pray.

Myra had no idea how long she sat on the couch, an hour, more, possibly less, until the spasms abated, the leg cramps eased up, and her breathing had leveled off. She marveled that no one had come to her aid; no one had asked her if she was all right. And there was no sign of Enrico. In the end, she decided that was a good thing. She told herself travelers were only concentrating on themselves and getting to where they needed to go. Stopping to help someone interfered with their personal agendas.

The crowd in the restroom was thinning out now. From past experience, Myra knew that airport restrooms the world over, especially the women's restrooms, were always the busiest when a flight arrived, then again right before a flight took off. If she could just hold out for another ten or fifteen minutes, she was almost certain the restroom would be down to one or two travelers.

Myra waited some more, taking shallow breaths. She began to feel strength returning, and her breathing was almost back to normal now. Her lungs no longer felt like they were on fire, and she could draw a deep breath.

Still, she waited. A full ten minutes before she got up and headed to the last stall in the long row. The handicapped stall with extra room, enough to accommodate a wheelchair. She entered on wobbly legs. She sat down and pulled up her shirt to rip at the duct tape. She squeezed her eyes shut, said a prayer that she would see the two bars she'd seen the last time. She debated a long moment as to the reception inside where she was. Did she dare turn it on? Maybe better to wait till she could get outside. In the end, she decided to wait. She strapped the phone back onto her waist and exited the stall.

At the sink she cupped her hand under the water and drank her fill. She was surprised to see she had the entire bathroom to herself. She winced when she saw her reflection in the mirror. Her hair was standing straight in the air. Her face looked dry and parched. And full of wrinkles. God, who was this person? She washed her face and hands, and did her best to finger-comb her hair. She spotted a small bottle of lotion someone had left behind. She drained the bottle, and lathered up her face and hands. The mirror told her that nothing had changed, but the skin on her face felt less taut and dry.

Myra walked over to the leather bench and

sat down. She needed a plan. She had to focus. *Think, Myra, think! Mission mode.* She had to get out of here. To someplace safe, so she could contact Charles or somehow make it to the American embassy. Charles always said in a foreign country when they were on a mission that the embassy was off-limits because it would call attention to them. If only she had her backpack and the special gold shield. If only . . .

The solution to her problem walked through the door a few minutes later in the form of a young woman wearing a straw hat with colorful streamers hanging down the sides and back. She was wheeling a small travel bag and had a backpack over her shoulders. She wobbled forward toward the sinks, singing a song in Spanish. Myra pegged her as a free spirit, with tats covering her arms and too many piercings to count. She was also drunk as a skunk.

Myra knew what she had to do even though it went against the grain. This was survival of the fittest. Hers.

Myra walked over to the young woman, took her arm, and led her over to the leather couch. "Oh, my dear, let me help you. You look exhausted." The woman smiled at her and giggled as Myra led her to the leather bench. You just sit here for a minute, dear. Let me get you some water. You look . . . ah . . . peaked, as my mother used to say."

"My mum used to say that, too. I'd rather have some gin," the young woman singsonged in a British accent.

"Okay, let me see if I can find some. Just sit

there and close your eyes. It might take me a little while to find some. Then we can party. Is that okay with you?" The young woman giggled again, her head bobbing up and down.

Luck stayed with Myra as she walked over to the sink. She heard a sound, then turned around in time to see the young girl fall over onto the leather bench. Myra rushed back, stripped off the backpack, then straightened the girl, so she was stretched out on the bench. She was snoring lightly.

God does work in mysterious ways, Myra thought as she raced to the closest stall, where she unzipped the backpack. A name tag sewn onto the lining said the owner of the backpack was Astrid Lansing. She lived in London, England. Myra rifled through the contents. *The Mother Lode.* Cell phone. Charger. Wallet. Keys. Credit cards. Nonprescription sunglasses. A book of traveler's checks. Passport. A change of clothes. Makeup bag. Two power bars. A bottle of flavored water.

Myra looked in the wallet. For sure, someone was smiling on her. She counted out $300 in American money and another two hundred in euros. Vacation money. Party money. She checked the phone and found that it was fully charged. She felt like she'd just won the lottery.

Myra peeled off her shirt and pulled on a madras plaid shirt from the backpack. She marveled at the perfect fit. At last, something was going her way. The straw hat the girl was wearing would work as a decent disguise. At least she hoped it would.

She walked out of the stall, the backpack over her shoulders. She ignored an elderly lady and a young teenage girl at the sink. Grandmother and granddaughter. They paid no attention to her, and she continued to ignore them as she trotted over to the sleeping young woman. She picked up the straw hat and plopped it on her head. She bent low, and whispered, "I'm really sorry about this, Astrid. I will make it up to you as soon as I can. Sleep well, my fairy godmother."

Myra was in full mission mode now as she walked out of the restroom to roam the concourse in search of an exit. She followed the crowds of travelers and eventually made it through to the outdoors. No one followed her. No one tried to stop her.

Safe.

For now.

Myra headed to the taxi line, waited her turn, and slid into the backseat. In her best rusty Spanish, she said, "Take me to the nearest hotel, please."

Chapter 6

"Run, Myra, run!" Annie screamed at the top of her lungs as she was pushed violently into the waiting car.

Enrico scrambled in behind her. "*Vamos*," he bellowed as he slammed Annie back against the seat. "No more nice guy, Countess."

Emboldened with Myra's getaway, Annie said, "Just for the record, Enrico, I never for a single moment thought you were a nice guy. You're a thug, a hoodlum, a bastard child with no real heritage. Your father wasn't a nice guy, either. He was weak, he lived off women, he had affairs and children all over the globe. All on my dime. He supported you and your mother on *my* money. Your mother was nothing more than a used woman who gave him three sons. None of you are worth a good spit. Of course, I didn't find that out till after he died." Sarcasm rang in her voice as she continued to screech as loud as she could, hoping for a reaction from her captor. When it came it was exactly what she had hoped for.

"Shut your mouth! My mother was a saint! I won't hear you blacken her name."

Aha, Annie thought, *his mother is his Achilles heel.* So she decided to go full bore. What did she have to lose at this stage of the game? She flipped the pages in Kathryn's playbook till she found the one she wanted. "Saint my ass! Your *mother* allowed your father to turn her into a whore with unlimited perks. A mistress, if for some obscure reason you like that term better. She liked the fine house he provided, the good food, designer clothes, jewelry, and all she had to do was spread her legs. After all, he was a *count*!

"All your mother had to do was keep popping out those babies to keep him coming back. And I had the honor of paying for it all. You and your brothers were born on the wrong side of the blanket, Enrico, face it. Nothing can change that! Nothing! You and your brothers are bastards, your mother was a whore, and your father was simply a sperm donor!" Annie continued to screech at the top of her lungs. She silently apologized to God for what she was saying. Later, if later ever came for her, she would find a way to atone for the ugly things she was saying. But for now, she had to survive doing whatever she could so that she could walk away alive and well.

Annie saw the raised hand, the murderous

fury in Enrico's eyes. She knew what was coming. She squared her shoulders to take the
blow. It was true, she thought crazily, when the
blow landed solidly on her right cheekbone,
you really do see stars. And then she slumped
over.

When she woke, she had no idea how much
time had passed. She was groggy but awake
enough that she felt herself being dragged
over what she thought was a flagstone walkway.
It was totally dark, with only a faint yellow light
coming from somewhere ahead. When she
stumbled and went down to her knees, Enrico
picked her up in a fireman's carry and hustled
her into what she thought of, at first glance, as a
very small house, a cottage at best. He dumped
her unceremoniously onto a flowered sofa. She
made no move to sit up, but she did stare up at
Enrico, her eyes burning with hatred.

A woman appeared out of nowhere, a little
woman with white hair and a deeply wrinkled
face. She was wearing a shapeless dress, with a
white apron over it. Her eyes burned with
something Annie couldn't define. The woman
glared at Enrico, then at Annie. She didn't
know *how* she knew, but she was absolutely certain that there was no love lost between these
two.

She stored that thoughtful nugget deep in
her mind. Enrico ordered the woman to make
coffee and to lace it with brandy. "For our
guest," he said in an ugly tone.

"Another relative living off my largesse?"

Annie asked snidely. "Who is she, and what is this place?" she asked boldly. "Where are we?"

"While it is none of your business, I will tell you anyway. The woman is my aunt Sophia. She is my mother's younger sister by one year. She nursed my mother night and day until she passed away. She prayed at her side and along with her. As my brothers and I did, too. Yes, my father, the sperm donor as you call him, bought this house for my aunt many years ago when I was still a small boy. He paid her to watch over us while he was away. He wanted to make sure we were all well taken care of. He was a kind man; he loved us and cared about us, this man you call a sperm donor."

"No. No, he was not a kind man, Enrico. I should know, I was married to him. He was a gigolo, a manipulator. He fooled me just the way he fooled your mother. He thought he was entitled to live like a king on my money because he was, after all, royalty, a *count*! A penniless count, to be sure.

"I had no idea the lengths he went to until after he died. My financial people were horrified at the millions and millions that he squandered. I realize that doesn't say much for me, but I did have a few illusions where he was concerned. I hated to give them up, but in the end, numbers do not lie. You may find this hard to believe, but I am glad that he at least provided for you and your family. Think about all the other families where he squatted that didn't fare so well. What's that saying, love 'em and leave 'em? Something like that." Annie couldn't help but notice how closely Sophia was listening to her words. She noted a spark of something in the woman's eyes but had no idea what it meant. Was it possible this woman could be an ally?

"Enough of this bullshit! I don't believe a word you're saying. If that's your story and what makes you happy, so be it. I know what I know," Enrico sputtered in the same ugly tone.

"Then you are an utter fool," Annie said wearily. "If all you believe is true, just ask yourself why your father didn't divorce me and make an honest woman of your mother. Stop lying to yourself, Enrico. Accept what is and get on with your life. I could be wrong about this, but I don't see the zeal you have in your two brothers. What? Because you are the oldest you have to . . . what . . . make yourselves legitimate? That's impossible. You can't prove Armand was your father. All the pictures of your fairy-tale life will not work in a court of law.

"One indisputable legal fact is that, until the day he died, I was married to the man you thought was your uncle. The world that you lived in believed Armand was your *uncle.* Your uncle. Not your father. There is no DNA to match against yours! Therefore, no proof. You need proof. *Rock-solid proof.* You do not have that.

"What you're doing is blackmailing me. You kidnapped me and my friend. That in itself is a serious offense. Thank God Myra got away;

she'll go to the authorities, to the American embassy, and they will hunt you down. Your days are numbered, Enrico. We are Americans, wealthy Americans, and our people will come after you with a vengeance.

"You threatened the padre and the whole village. Those people will testify against you. That's against the law also. You are trying to extort money from me. That is also against the law. You can't win, don't you see that? Even if you kill me, you won't win. You and your brothers will never see a penny of my money. This is all for nothing.

"Let me go. I'll go back to America and pretend this never happened." Annie knew she was wasting her breath, but she had to try. It was only a small effort compared to what Myra had done.

"Save your breath, Countess. Unless you give me what I want, you have no other option but to reconcile yourself to living out the rest of your days in this house under lock and key. They will never find you," he thundered. "Yes, my aunt is old and no match for your strength, but there will be guards outside. As you Americans like to say, you are doomed."

"Like I don't already know that," Annie muttered under her breath. *It's all on you, Myra. All on you. Please, make it happen. Get me out of here.*

While Annie was coming to terms with what lay ahead of her, Myra walked outside of her hotel room onto a tiny balcony. She wondered how safe she really was here. On her arrival, the desk clerk had given her a very hard time because she didn't have a passport to turn over. He had gone on and on about how the hostel was for students, and it was clear she wasn't a student. His English was good enough that he took pity on her when she said she was a teacher with a group who had gotten mugged and robbed. She asked him how to get to the U.S. Consulate, and he'd written out instructions, but not until one hundred dollars in U.S. currency changed hands. He was also smart enough to ask what she was doing with a backpack if she had gotten mugged and robbed. She'd forced tears of frustration to trickle down her cheeks when she said she had simply picked the bag up off the ground when the students ran off. He'd looked skeptical, but in the end he allowed her to register.

Myra decided she was safe for another few hours, possibly a day, after which she would have to make a move.

Myra leaned on the balcony railing and closed her eyes. She was so tired. And hungry. She couldn't remember the last time she'd eaten. She did not remember the huge breakfast she had had with the two priests. All she could remember was that she had waved the airline dinner away when the hostess tried to set it in front of her. She didn't want to get airsick. Instead, she'd nibbled on a small bag of stale pretzels. She'd accepted the little carton of apple juice. Her stomach started to grind, reminding her again of how hungry she was. She was probably also dehydrated, which would account for her light-headed feeling. She closed her eyes again and wished she were back at Pinewood.

Myra gave herself a mental shake, opened her eyes, and stared out at the darkness. She couldn't see a moon, and only a few stars twinkled overhead. Down below, she watched traffic on what looked to be a two-lane road that probably led into town. In the distance, she could see pinpricks of light everywhere. They reminded her of the fireflies back at Pinewood on warm summer evenings. She blinked away her tears of frustration.

Myra looked down at the special phone that was in her hand. Her lifeline. She was so relieved to see the two bars winking at her that she grew even more light-headed. She knew what the bars meant on a regular cell phone but was unsure what they signified on this special phone that was, she thought, satellite driven. Always powered up was what she had been led to believe by Avery Snowden. Unless there was no satellite overhead. She'd give up everything she owned right now to know that the old spy and his operatives were here in Spain, looking for her. Maybe someday she would understand it, but right now all she could do was think about calling Charles.

Myra's hands were sweaty. She wiped one first on her jeans, then the other, transferring the precious phone from left to right. She needed to calm down, she needed a steady hand. She clicked the number one and waited. Nothing.

Damn. She waited a minute and tried again. Still nothing. She ran back into the room to get Astrid Lansing's phone, which was fully charged. It looked just like her personal Verizon phone, which Enrico had confiscated. But it bore a carrier she'd never heard of. She knew the country code for the United States, so she pressed in the numbers. She was thankful the phone apparently didn't need a password. The call went immediately to voice mail.

Myra started to babble like a three-year-old on steroids. She wound down by giving the name of the youth hostel where she was and Astrid's cell number. "I'll wait here for you to get to me, Charles. You have to hurry, they have Annie, and I don't know where they took her. At first we thought they weren't killers, but I don't think that anymore, Charles. I'm afraid for Annie. Hurry, please."

Myra was so emotionally drained that she trudged back to the small room and plopped down on the bed. She hoped the reason Charles didn't pick up was because he was on his way to rescue her. She absolutely would not believe he didn't pick up because he didn't recognize the British cell phone carrier.

Exhausted, Myra closed her eyes and fell asleep with Astrid Lansing's cell phone clutched in her hand, unaware that Astrid had turned the phone to vibrate instead of ringing in preparation for boarding a flight. Or disembarking, whatever the case was.

* * *

It wasn't until they were through Customs and their bags loaded into the long stretch van that Charles pulled out his cell phone. Six calls, none of them important enough to hold up the drive. He squinted at the last call, trying to figure out the number since it was a UK number. He held up his hand to stop everything and for quiet. He listened to the message, a smile spreading from ear to ear. He could hear the group's collective sigh of relief at his expression.

"That was Myra. She called on a phone that she stole from some drunk young woman. Along with her money and clothes. That's my girl! She got away from the men holding Annie captive. She's off the mountain in a small youth hostel. I have the name. The bad guys still have Annie. The bad guys are Annie's husband's illegitimate children. They want her fortune. That's the bottom line."

Suddenly, everyone was talking at once. Questions peppered the air, but all Charles could say was, "I told you everything Myra said; beyond that I know nothing. All we can do now is speculate. Myra is waiting for us to pick her up. She sounded tired and worried and frightened. And yet she managed to get away. That's my girl!" Charles said, and the second time, it sounded prouder.

"Are you going to call her?" Yoko asked.

Charles was already dialing the number that appeared on the screen. He winced when the call went straight to voice mail. He drew in a mighty breath and let it out. "We're here, old girl, we're coming to get you, so sit tight. We just have to figure out where your youth hostel is compared to where we are. Do not, I repeat, do not leave your hotel."

Charles turned to the girls, and said, "I'm thinking Myra does not know the cell owner's password to retrieve messages or how that particular phone works that she has in her possession. Of course, I could be wrong, but my thinking is she's glued to that phone waiting for me to get back to her. Nothing else makes sense. We need a map."

"I have one right here," Maggie said. "Doesn't look too far from where we are. The address Myra gave you in Barcelona is centrally located and is near to Las Ramblas and Plaça de Catalunya. There are a couple of student reviews that say the shared bathrooms could be cleaner, but they are understaffed. The price for a night is $23 American. Which, by the way, is kind of pricey for a youth hostel that usually goes from ten to twelve bucks a night with breakfast included. Just saying.

"And before you can ask, we're booked at the Oriente Atiram, Las Ramblas, and it's right on Las Ramblas Boulevard. Says it is a two-minute walk to their metro station. That's good to know, I'm thinking." No one disagreed.

"What are we waiting for, then? Let's go!" Nikki said.

The gang scrambled aboard the oversize van, with Ted at the wheel.

"Hold on, people, I have a text coming in from Avery," Charles said. Everyone stopped in their tracks while Charles read the tiny words on his phone.

"Avery is here. He said he is right in the heart of town and will meet us at the center of Las Ramblas at an open-air café. He said he'll find us if we leave now."

Ted tapped the horn lightly, and yelled, "All aboard. Next stop, Myra's digs!"

Everyone's arm shot high in the air as they scrambled to their seats to buckle up.

Ted waited impatiently for the fast-moving traffic to slow long enough for him to inch his way onto the busy thoroughfare. Espinosa rode shotgun, with the understanding that he would do all the talking if Spanish was required with anyone they would need to converse with.

"So what's our game plan?" Jack asked.

Charles called over his shoulder. "First, we pick up Myra. Then we head to town to meet up with Avery, after which we will go to the hotel that Maggie secured for us and check in. After that, we will listen to what Myra has to tell us, at which point we'll formulate a plan to get Annie out of the situation she is in and back among us.

"According to the map, Maggie, how far to our destination, meaning the youth hostel?" Ted called over his shoulder.

Maggie stared down at the local map on her computer. "This is just a guess on my part, an hour, maybe a little more."

"We're off to the races, people," Ted bellowed.

* * *

Myra rolled over, sighed, then opened her eyes. This was definitely not the most comfortable bed she'd ever slept in. The fact of the matter was that she hadn't slept in a twin bed since she was seven years old. She was amazed that she hadn't fallen onto the floor. Back home, she had a California king bed that she dearly loved. She looked at her watch. She'd slept through the night. She could see dawn starting to break through the window. She still felt tired.

Myra's thoughts immediately flew to Annie and her safety. And then on to Charles. Maybe he had called. She looked at Astrid Lansing's cell phone and felt the vibration. Then she swore, words that even Kathryn probably didn't know. Charles might have called while she slept and she would have missed his call because the phone was set to vibration mode. She noticed a blinking red light. Since the phone had been fully charged, the light must mean there were messages or texts to be retrieved. How to retrieve them? She had no clue, so she tried everything she would have tried on her American cell phone, with no results other than to see the number 23 pop up on the screen. That had to mean Astrid had 23 messages or texts. For a young woman, she supposed that was par for the course. Without a password, though, Myra knew she would get nowhere with the cell phone.

Now, what should she do? How would she know if Charles had returned her call or not?

She wouldn't, was the answer she gave herself. Maybe what she needed to do was go to whatever passed for a town and see if her satellite phone would work there. Why, she asked herself, did everything go wrong just when you so desperately needed it to go right? Since there was no answer to that question either, Myra plopped Astrid Lansing's straw hat with the colorful streamers on her head and left the room, still in the clothes she'd slept in. She wished she had time for a shower, but time was of the essence.

In the small lobby, Myra looked at her surroundings because she really hadn't paid much attention when she arrived. Then all she wanted was a safe room with a lock on the door. There were no frills in this hostel. It was spartan, to say the least. The lobby, if that's what it was, was long and narrow, with four chairs that looked reasonably comfortable and a table with outdated magazines and newspapers, all in Spanish. The floors were Spanish tile, a reddish copper color, and the walls were cream colored. Pictures of outdoor scenes, all rendered in green and yellow, graced the walls. Local talent, she surmised. A tired-looking plant whose leaves were more yellow than green, and badly in need of water, stood next to the only window in the room.

Before she entered the lobby, Myra craned her neck to see if the desk clerk was behind the desk. Right now, she didn't want any questions or conversation. When she didn't see anyone, she went directly for the door, and the moment she was outside, she turned left for no reason other than that was the direction the other pedestrians were going. She fell in line and meandered along, ever watchful. No one seemed to pay any attention to her. Astrid Lansing's backpack was on her back.

Twenty minutes into her walk, Myra spotted a line of outdoor cafés, bistros, and tourist shops featuring souvenirs. She entered the first café she came to and looked around. She had to reach out to grasp hold of the back of a chair when she felt a wave of dizziness sweep over her. She needed to eat and drink *NOW*. She sat down, shook her head, and asked for a glass of water, which she consumed in three long gulps. She asked for another glass of water and a pot of coffee. Not a cup, a pot, she said clearly, so there was no mistake. Then she pointed to a picture on the wall of a plate filled a foot high with pancakes.

Her head clearer now that she had finished off the second glass of water, she realized that her first mistake, which Avery Snowden had drilled into all their heads, was that she was sitting with her back to an open doorway. Always know where your exits are and how many there are. Always have a clear line of sight. She immediately moved quickly to a table farther back in the room. The waiter, a young man of maybe sixteen or so, looked puzzled, but Myra just smiled at him.

Only one exit, the one she'd walked in through. One window, with a luscious-looking green plant hanging in the center, impeding the view beyond.

Myra's coffee arrived. At last. As far as she could remember, it had been days since she'd had any coffee. She could barely contain herself when she poured from a full carafe. Nothing in her life had ever tasted as good as the coffee she was drinking. It was dark, robust, with possibly a hint of chicory in it. She drank two full cups, straight up, no cream or sugar. She thought she could feel the caffeine course through her entire body.

Two full glasses of water and two full cups of coffee demanded she head to the restroom, which was surprisingly clean and even pretty, with fresh flowers on the vanity sink. Myra washed her hands, splashed water on her face, and actually started to feel a bit like her old self.

When she took her seat at the small table in the back of the room, she was stunned to see her breakfast waiting for her. This was a Maggie Spritzer breakfast, not a Myra Rutledge breakfast. She counted eight pancakes dripping with golden butter and thick syrup. Nestled alongside the pancakes were four generous-sized sausage patties. There was no way on earth she could eat all that was on the oversize plate. No way.

She was wrong. When she finished eating, the only thing remaining on her plate was one sausage patty and a small puddle of syrup. The coffee carafe was empty.

Myra paid the bill, $7 in U.S. dollars. When she walked out of the café, she felt like a million bucks and ready to take on the world. She looked around, practicing what Avery Snowden had taught his pupils, tradecraft. Always know where you are, always be aware of your surroundings, know the path to take if you need to elude someone, keep your eyes on the people around you, do they look like they belong or not belong? There's always a "tell" if someone doesn't belong. Never look over your shoulder. Instead, listen to footsteps if there are no storefronts where you can window-shop and still see what's behind you. She remembered it all and did everything she was supposed to do. That's when she saw the large white van. It didn't look like it belonged. All the other cars were small Fiats and, of course, the mopeds clogging the narrow road. The van was creeping along behind a string of mopeds. She could see it in the window of a shop that sold handmade boots.

Myra strained to see ahead of her for any similar-looking vehicles. There were none. *It doesn't belong.* Somehow, Enrico and his people had found her. Avery's warning rang in her ears. "Do not panic. Assess the situation. Remove yourself from the situation. If you only have a split second to make a decision, go with your gut." Myra whirled around and started back the way she had come. She didn't look back, but she could see through the streamers hanging from her straw hat that she was almost alongside the large van. "Don't run," Avery had said. "Don't run but move as fast as you can." Normally, Myra could move as fast as the others, but not after the monster breakfast she'd just consumed. She cursed the stack of pancakes she'd just eaten.

Just move, Myra, just move. She heard a sound then, a sound she was familiar with, a panel door on a van sliding across. *Run!* Her mind shrieked. *Run!* Directly in her path was an elderly man walking two large dogs, so she couldn't run even if she wanted to. She stepped aside and pressed herself up against a plateglass window. When the man and the dogs swept past her, she ran; but she wasn't fast enough. She felt strong arms grab her from behind. She screamed at the top of her lungs as she tried to jerk free as the straw hat with the streamers was ripped off her head.

"Jack! Oh, my God! Jack, is it really you?"

"Yeah, yeah, it's me. Will you just shut up already, Myra, or people are going to think I'm kidnapping you. It's me, it's really me. We're all here in the white van. Myra, shut up, okay?"

Myra clamped her lips tight.

She knew how to follow orders.

Chapter 7

Myra felt herself being pushed and shoved toward the van, the straw hat with the streamers clutched in her hands. She gulped at the air like a fish out of water as willing hands pulled and pushed at her. She heard people shouting, "GO!" And then the white van was moving, its horn blasting the vehicles and the hordes of mopeds in front to get out of the way.

"Easy, old girl, easy," Charles crooned as he stroked Myra's hair, which was damp with perspiration. Everyone was talking and shouting and trying to get close enough to hug her. "You're safe now. Everything is going to be okay. We're on our way to meet with Avery. Easy now, luv. Deep breaths."

Myra took a huge, deep breath and let it out slowly as tears rolled down her cheeks. "They have Annie. I don't know if I should have stayed with her or not," she gasped. "I saw a chance to run, and I took it. We have to find her. The man is a maniac; he's going to do something bad to her if she doesn't do what he wants. I don't know where he took her," Myra wailed. "I just ran and ran. I still can't believe he didn't come after me. He's going to make Annie pay for it."

"We'll find her, Myra," Charles said soothingly. "We won't give up till we find her."

"Promise, Charles. Promise we'll find her."

"I promise," Charles said solemnly.

A weak smile tugged at the corners of Myra's lips when everyone in the van echoed Charles's words. And then the questions came laser fast, with Myra trying to keep up. When she realized she was babbling incoherently, she threw her hands up in the air just as Jack whistled sharply for silence.

"Okay, people, one at a time. Myra," he said gently, "slow and easy wins the race. Take your time, we have all day," Jack said.

"No, Jack, we don't have all day. Annie is in that man's hands. He is not a nice man, either. He wants what he wants, and he won't stop till he gets it. Annie is at his mercy, and I don't know where he took her. This is his country. We're at a severe disadvantage. I should never have made a run for it. Oh, God, why did I do that? I left her! I left Annie behind!" Myra cried.

"You're wrong, luv. You did exactly what we were all trained to do. Any one of us, and that includes Annie, would have done the same thing. Running as you did gives us a fighting chance. Avery's entire team is here. He'll leave no stone unturned. He'll enlist the aid of the locals.

"We can't rush into anything. Annie is safe for the moment. If you're thinking he's going to harm her, you're wrong. He needs her, and Annie is no fool, she knows that. She'll do whatever she needs to do."

"She's never going to forgive me for leaving her. Never. She has nothing, they took everything. All she has is her wits and . . . and . . ."

"You said, did you not, that when you bolted, she screamed, 'Run, Myra, run!' That's the proof that she wanted you to do what you did. She's counting on your finding us and our finding her. Trust me, knowing Annie as I do, she is figuring all the angles. If I were a betting man, which I am at times, my money would be on Annie. We're thinking positive, here, luv," Charles said gently.

Myra's head bobbed up and down, just as a symphony of sound hit the roof of the van. She doubled over, her eyes wild. "Gunshots! Oh, my God, they found us!"

"No, no, no! It's rain," Nikki said. "The sky just opened up. Look outside, Myra. It's just rain."

Myra went slack in Charles's arms. "I'm . . . ah . . . just a tad twitchy. I'm sorry."

"This rain is a good thing," Ted called over his shoulder. "All the mopeds ahead are looking for cover. Does everyone in this country drive a moped?" he asked to no one in particular. No one answered him, so he concentrated on trying to see through the heavy downpour, with windshield wipers that were less than efficient going as fast as they could.

"Do we have a plan?" Myra asked.

"Not yet. Once we meet up with Avery and get to our hotel, we'll get down to work," Charles said. "I want you to relax now. We'll go through all the questions and answers when we're behind closed doors. Are you listening to me, Myra?"

"Of course I'm listening to you, Charles. What you all need to do is listen to *ME*."

"And we will, luv, just as soon as we can get settled. For now, we all just want you to calm down and relax. You better than anyone know what can happen when you strike out without a solid foundation. This is Annie we're talking about. The one thing I am really grateful for is that you did not go to the American embassy. That's the first place people like Annie's captors will be watching. We need to be extra careful and cautious here, luv, as this is not our country, and we're starting off at a serious disadvantage. Tell me you understand."

Myra's head bobbed up and down.

"Good. Now try to relax."

"Okay, people, we are approaching the square. If Snowden is out there, I can't see him through this heavy rain. What do you want me to do? Should I park in the hope that he will see us first or what?" Ted asked.

Everyone had a comment. The end result was that they parked as close to the square as possible, with Dennis and Espinosa getting out to look around.

The mother in Myra surfaced. "No, don't get out, boys. It's a cold rain, and you'll get a chill and get sick. Just park. Avery will find us. You can always call him, Charles."

Charles chuckled. "Now, why didn't I think of that! Thank you, dear, for being so insightful and reminding me of my position here."

While Charles took care of business, Myra lowered her voice to a whisper, and said, "I am so worried about Annie. I just know she's going to do something that is going to get her in more trouble than she's in now. She's furious. I don't think she's going to wait for us to find her. It's just a feeling I have, one that I can't shake."

Everyone was stunned when Harry spoke up. "Annie is no fool. She knows the score. She won't do anything rash. She'll watch and bide her time until she thinks the moment is right to make a move. Show some faith in her abilities. It's amazing what people can do when their life is in danger. Look what you did, Myra."

The group simply stared at Harry, who was not known for talking or giving speeches. They all nodded as Yoko patted her husband on the head. Harry beamed his pleasure.

The van turned silent just as Charles ended his call. Cyrus barked to show he was ready for some *action*.

"We're to follow that gaggle of mopeds over to the right, Ted. At least they have ponchos on. They'll lead the way. Avery said the only way to move around here is by moped, as we've just learned. They're going to lead us to our hotel. He said it's about fifteen minutes from where we are right now."

"We should make good time then," Ted shouted, "because the road ahead is clear as far as I can see. Maybe we should ditch this set of wheels and go with mopeds ourselves."

"To be discussed at the hotel," Charles shot back.

Ted shrugged. "Easy for you to say; you aren't driving in this unholy mess. Have any of you noticed how narrow these roads are? This is not your average vehicle, as you can see compared to those minicars out there. The darn thing takes up the whole road. I'm not complaining; I'm just saying."

"It's raining harder," Maggie said, just to have something to say.

The van went quiet again as Ted followed the moped brigade.

Cyrus let loose with a yip that said he wasn't a happy camper, but he'd endure since he was scrunched between Jack and Nikki.

Myra suddenly reared up, her eyes wild. "Oh, Charles, I broke my pearls. Annie said I had to break them so we could leave a trail of bread crumbs so you all would know we were on the mountain when you came to rescue us. I didn't want to do it, but I didn't have a choice. We need to go back to the mountain so I can try to find them. I can't . . . I . . . what will

I do without my pearls? They're part of my life. I can't believe I . . ." Tears welled in her eyes at her loss.

It wasn't Charles who consoled Myra at the loss of her beloved pearls but the girls and Cyrus, who tried to lick at her tears. The girls promised that they would go back and get on their hands and knees to scour the ground. "Cyrus will sniff them out," Nikki said. "We'll get them back, I promise, Myra," Nikki said.

Cyrus yipped his approval. Sniffing for pearls was *action* of a sort.

Ted steered the huge van around a curve, then maneuvered his way forward to what looked like a quaint gabled inn that was exquisitely landscaped. Ted parked and pressed a lever that opened the side doors. Everyone clambered outside, backpacks and luggage in tow. Cyrus danced around, yipping and yapping his happiness to have his four legs on solid ground. He nudged Jack forward, his sign that he had business to take care of.

Avery meandered over to them and saluted smartly. "Welcome to Spain, ladies and gentlemen. This is a small hotel. I engaged every room. The owners have a communal room that they rent out for social occasions, and that comes with our rental. Let us all check in and meet there in an hour. Get your passports ready. I'll take care of things."

Myra hung back and pressed Charles's arm to step to the side. "I don't have my passport. That man took it. He also took my special gold shield. He has Annie's, too. How am I going to register?" she asked fearfully.

"You're a guest of mine. A visitor. You are not a guest of the hotel. There is a difference. Just stay in the crowd. They'll match the room to the passport. Try to relax, dear. I need you to be you. You can handle all this. I promise that we will find Annie. I promise that we will find your beloved pearls. And you know that I have never broken a promise to you."

"Oh, Charles, what would I do without you?"

Charles grinned. "I can't believe you said that to me. Just look back at all you've done in the past few days, and I was nowhere in evidence. You did it all on your own. And now we're together. End of story."

"You left out the part that I am also a thief. I have to make it right for that young woman, Astrid Lansing, as soon as possible. I want to make sure she gets this hat back. For some reason, I think it was special to her. I robbed her, Charles. I did that!"

"Of course you did, but you did not harm her. It was a question of survival. Yours. Any one of us would have done the same thing. You will make it right in the end, and that young lady will have tales to spin for her friends for years to come."

Myra leaned into Charles's arms. "You always know the right thing to say to me. Thank you, my darling husband."

Charles hugged his wife tight to his side. "It looks like we're checked in. Stay close to me and mix with the others."

"This is one of those times when I'm glad you're on the portly side, dear," Myra smiled.

"Portly is it?"

"Oh, you know what I mean, Charles. If you were a string bean of a man like Ted, I wouldn't be able to hide behind you."

In spite of himself, Charles laughed out loud. One look from Avery Snowden was all Charles needed to turn solemn and serious.

Snowden took the lead to the ancient-looking elevator. He pointed to a corridor on the right. "That's the communal room where we'll meet up in an hour."

In the cozy room nestled under the eaves with the door closed, Myra collapsed into Charles's arms. She cried then, great gulping sobs as she swiped at her eyes with the sleeve of Astrid Lansing's shirt, which she was wearing. She apologized for crying between sobs. "I feel so guilty that I left Annie. If anything happens to her, it will be my fault. God, Charles, how will I be able to live with that?"

Charles gently pushed Myra so that she was facing him. "Listen to me, Myra. It's okay to cry until you can't cry anymore. Tears are cathartic. What is not all right is for you to blame yourself. I promise you that we will find Annie. I promise, Myra. I've never made a promise to you, ever, that I did not keep. We will find her, and it might not be on your immediate timetable, but we will be successful."

"I know, I know. I hear everything you're saying, and I believe you, but . . . but until that happens, that man can . . . he can hurt Annie. What if . . ."

"There are no what-ifs. We *will* find her, and when we do, Annie will be the victor. I know in my gut that, wherever she is, she is planning her escape. You have to put your faith in Annie."

"I am more than a little worried that Enrico, that's his name, Enrico, he has our gold shields. What if he figures out . . . Good Lord, I can't even bring myself to say out loud what he could do with not one but two of those shields."

A tentative knock sounded on the door. Charles opened it. Nikki handed over a pile of clothing for Myra. Charles simply nodded. The Sisters took care of one another.

Myra smiled as she reached for the pile of clothing. She almost swooned at the thought of taking a shower and washing her hair, then putting on clean clothes. She nodded as she made her way to the tiny bathroom that was blindingly clean. She hoped the water was hot and steamy.

The shower was all Myra could have hoped for. The water was hot, the soap lemony, and the complimentary mini-bottle of shampoo smelled like fresh peaches and vanilla. The complimentary toothbrush did double duty as Myra brushed and scrubbed. Satisfied that she was good to go, she walked out of the bathroom, feeling better than she'd felt in days. She looked at Charles and smiled.

"I feel like my old self, Charles. Thank you for bringing me up short. I'm sorry for the tears. No, no, I'm not sorry. I needed to cry. And you're right, tears are cathartic. You're right about something else, too. Annie will fight and make things go her way. She has the advantage of knowing Enrico by now since she has been his captive for three long months. She'll figure out something. She will, Charles. I know this. Go along now, the bathroom is all yours. I'll be fine. I *am* fine, dear."

"Yes, dear. Bossy bossy," Charles said, chuckling.

Myra didn't respond; she just nodded, her thoughts having moved on to Astrid Lansing and to Annie. But this time with a new perspective. Her eyes narrowed when she thought about what she and the Sisters would do to Enrico Araceli when they found him. Not *if* they found him but *when*.

Twenty minutes later, Myra and Charles followed Avery Snowden into the hotel's communal room. The others straggled in one by one, their expressions tense until the room was full. Extra folding chairs were brought in by the hotel staff. A huge silver urn of coffee along with what looked like delicious pastries sat invitingly on a sideboard, along with a heaping bowl of fruit.

Charles waited till everyone had coffee and pastries before he called the meeting to order. "Who wants to go first?"

Cyrus barked. Everyone laughed, the tension broken. Avery Snowden stood up and started to talk. "I don't have any answers at this moment for you all. I've reached out to some people here who I think can help us. They in turn know other people. You all know how that works. I do have some background information on Enrico Araceli and his two brothers. Newspaper stuff and the like. We're compiling a list of people to talk to: old neighbors, the mother's friends, the padre at the local church they all attended. We need time to schedule interviews and sort through it all. Enrico's mother, whose name was Elena, had a sister.

"Annie's husband, the count, was what, back in the States, we would call a big wheel over here. No one appears to have known that, though he was a count, he was actually penniless. This is something one of my operatives got from one of the locals, who knew the three sons. We have to put it all together. It's ongoing."

"What about the mountain?" Ted asked. "We tried to find out the name of it and struck out. It has to have a name."

"I did find out the name of the village at the bottom of that mountain. It's called the Village of Tears," Maggie said. "I Googled it, and there seem to be conflicting stories about how it came to have its name. One is that the monks all died off on the mountain, and the few who were left moved down off the mountain and set up the village. Another story was that the count's family lost all their money and had to move to the village and scrounge out a living. The third story was that the mountain was haunted, and bad things happened to the

people there, mainly the de Silva family. They
started dying off, one by one, until only
Annie's husband remained. He hightailed it
down the mountain, so the curse wouldn't get
him, and relocated to the village.

"With no money and nothing to back him
up, it's said, rumored actually, that he took off
to the city, where he proved himself an ab-
solute master at insinuating himself among
the rich and powerful. A gigolo, if you will. He
used his title to live off women."

Dennis felt like his eyes were going to bug
out of his head. He gasped out loud. "Maggie,
are you saying that Annie's husband was, in ef-
fect, a male prostitute?"

"I'm not saying it, Dennis. That's what I
found out, but yes, I think that's what Annie's
husband was."

Nikki looked around at the faces staring at
Maggie. She had to clear her throat several
times before she could get the words out. She
fixed her gaze on Myra. "Did Annie ever know
or find out?"

"She knew that he had been unfaithful to
her. That's why she took Elena and relocated
to Virginia, only going back to Spain in the
summers, so Armand could see Elena. After
Jonathan showed up, her people did some re-
search and discovered that Jonathan was not
his sister's child, as he had said—it seems he
had no siblings at all—but his own child from
a lady of the night.

"She didn't know anything about this until
Enrico kidnapped her and proceeded to en-

lighten her. She was absolutely devastated. She had no clue about their existence. Not a single one. He showed her an album. Annie told me she lost it. Right then and there. That's what she was dealing with for the three months he held her captive on the mountain. She said he would taunt her with the album. He kept telling her over and over that her husband used her money to take care of him, his brothers, and his mother. Uncle Armand, Enrico called him. But Annie came to accept all that he was telling her. Pictures don't lie; and then there is the fact that he looks exactly like Armand. Enrico even has the same mannerisms."

"How awful for Annie," Kathryn said. "It's beyond cruel."

Yoko dabbed at her eyes. Harry put his arm around her shoulders.

"If the man weren't already dead, I think I might take a crack at killing him," Alexis said through clenched teeth.

"Save the venom for Enrico and the brothers," Snowden suggested.

"You can count on it, Mr. Snowden," Kathryn barked.

The room went silent for a few minutes.

Finally, Jack broke the silence. "What's our next move? What can we do? We're a small army here. If we work in tandem, we should be able to come up with some good leads that will take us to wherever Annie is being held. Just tell us what to do."

"What did you find out about Enrico's mother?" Charles asked. "Seems to me that would be a good starting point. And you said she has a sister. Since the mother passed away, we should concentrate on everything we can find out about her. She's still alive, so she's living somewhere."

"Enrico said the sister took care of his mother until she passed away. Annie told me he said they prayed together. He seemed fond of his aunt, said she looked out for them growing up when *Uncle* Armand was away on business. She cooked and cleaned and saw to the boys. She was the person who taught them their catechism, took them to church. No clue what the mother did back then when she wasn't sick.

"Annie told me there were pictures of her in the album, and Annie said she was a beautiful woman, pictures of her decked out in designer outfits at various luncheons, parties, and the like. They all lived in a big, elegant house and wanted for nothing. There were several maids, a gardener, a fancy car with a chauffeur. Until Armand died. Then everything went down the drain, and they had to move out of the big, elegant house because there was no money.

"According to what Enrico told Annie, neither he nor his brothers had any idea about their *uncle's* double life. They knew nothing about Annie. The mother only told them what she knew on her deathbed."

"That just makes this whole mess worse," Isabelle said.

"Yes, it does," Myra said sadly.

Charles held up his hands for silence. "We

need to make a plan here. We can all separate and check out whomever you need us to talk to. We should be able to speed things up with all of us working together. I believe the sister will be the key. Someone has to know her. If she was a regular churchgoer, then I think that's where we should start. Tell us how you want to divide up the interviews."

Two hours later, the Sisters leaned back in their respective chairs and looked at one another.

Nikki took the lead. "We need to shelve the van and travel by moped. I'm sure the desk clerk can rent us some mopeds. We'll need maps. I don't know how much we can do before it gets dark. Kathryn and I have the padre. We're going to leave now before the dinner hour. We'll check back here by seven, when I think we should have dinner and retire for the night. I'm feeling the jet lag, and I know the rest of you are, too. Still, I recognize the fact that none of us will be able to sleep unless we physically do something today. Dennis, what is the hotel saying about the mopeds?"

"Ten minutes, and they'll all be here."

"I'm staying behind with Charles and Fergus," Myra said. "Mainly because I don't have any kind of identification." The group said they understood and departed for the lobby to wait for the arrival of the mopeds.

Myra called out. "The sister's name is Sophia. Annie said she has the same last name of Araceli as the mother."

When the door closed behind the Sisters and the boys, Myra turned around and asked, "Do we have an extra laptop?"

"No, but you can use mine," Fergus said. "I'm too wired up to work it. Myra, are you sure that Annie is okay?"

"She was right as rain when I took it on the lam. Don't go negative on me, Fergus. I can't handle it if you do. We all have to have faith in Annie. Do you hear me, Fergus?" Myra demanded shrilly.

"Yes, Myra, I hear you, and I am doing my best. I hope it's good enough."

"It has to be good enough, Fergus. It just has to be. Now, what's your password, so I can get to work?"

"What do you think it is? 'Countess,' of course."

"Of course it is." Myra grinned as she typed in the word.

Chapter 8

Annie struggled to sit upright on the flowered sofa. She looked around at the small room and marveled at how cozy it was. And clean. Armand had purchased this for the little woman wearing the white apron. Later, she would think about that. Now she had to focus. And listen. One could learn a lot by listening instead of talking. Charles had drilled that little fact into all their heads back in the day.

Annie tried to assess the little woman in the apron. Enrico had said something about her not being a match for Annie's strength. And yet, even with the white hair and the wrinkles, the woman seemed strong to Annie. And there was something in her eyes that did not speak of old age. Maybe it was how she moved. She didn't shuffle or trudge or plop. In fact, she seemed to glide over the polished floors. Maybe she was putting on an act for her nephew. Then again, maybe a lot of things, Annie thought in disgust.

"Coffee, señora," the old woman said as she set down a pretty china cup on a matching saucer. "These dishes once belonged to my sister," she said. Annie wanted the coffee desperately, but there was no way she was going to drink it. Another rule of Charles's, never eat or drink anything unless you know one hundred percent that it is safe. She shook her head.

Sophia tilted her head to the side. "It is safe to drink, señora. I made it. She pointed to the door and said, "Rico, no you do not drink."

Annie made an ugly noise in the back of her throat to show what she thought of that statement. She realized then how hungry she was. At that moment, she felt like she could chew a doorknob.

To prove her point, Sophia picked up the cup and took a healthy gulp. She then refilled the cup to the brim and handed the cup to Annie. "Trust me, señora."

And for some strange reason, Annie did trust her. She accepted the cup and drank greedily. Ah, nectar of the gods. She nodded at Sophia and handed her the cup.

"More, señora?" Annie nodded. Sophia poured generously. She was equally generous with the brandy bottle. "Are you hungry, señora? Of course you are," Sophia said, answering her own question. "I will fix you some food. It will be safe to eat. You can watch me prepare it.

Come with me to the kitchen and watch. If Rico comes in, say nothing. Nothing at all. Do you understand me, señora?" Annie nodded as her hopes rose. Maybe this woman would turn out to be an ally after all.

It was a country kitchen, with a fieldstone fireplace with almost a full wall of firewood stacked high. A fire burned brightly and was fragrant. A wide plank table with two benches took up the middle of the floor. She'd seen tables and benches like these back in the States at Pier One, where she loved to go to browse with Myra on Saturday afternoons. She slid onto one of the benches and looked around. There were some healthy-looking plants on the wide windowsills. A picture of a bright red teapot, which looked to be a child's painting, hung on a wall by the Dutch door. There were no cabinets or cupboards, just open shelves that held colored dishes and dried flower arrangements. A small radio sat on one of the shelves next to salt and pepper shakers. She'd seen no evidence of a television or computer. Nothing electronic. How did this woman communicate with the outside world? she wondered. Somewhere, someplace, there had to be a phone. There just had to be one. Annie cautioned herself to stay alert. Charles's words of "listen" rang over and over in her head. Listening, she told herself, was good; but in order to listen, there had to be a dialogue. She took the bull by the horns as she watched Sophia slice ham onto a yellow platter. "Where is this place?" she asked.

"In America, you would probably say you are in the country. We are fifty miles from the city. I am sorry to tell you this, señora, but no one knows I live here. Armand, your . . . your husband . . . he used another name on all the paperwork. I suspect now that was not the case at all. He told me the paperwork says I can live here until I die. It has been many years, and I have had no problems. After my death, I do not know what happens to this property."

How generous of you, Armand. For some reason, the news wasn't upsetting her. "How do you live? Do you have a job?" Annie asked, curious now.

"Rico gives me a pittance to live on. I raise chickens and sell the eggs in the village. I sell the figs, too. I barter with the villagers. I manage. I taught school for a short while but had to give it up. My job was to see to my sister and the boys. It is a family, the way things are done." Annie found herself blinking at the bitterness in Sophia's voice.

"Why didn't you rebel? Leave?"

"And go where and do what, señora? This is not the United States. Rico would not allow it. Nor would Armand. My sister . . . she was very demanding. I had no choice. Before you can ask, yes, I regret all of that. Now that I am old, I no longer care. I live here. I paint pictures. Sometimes I sell them in the village to tourists. I have a garden, I can vegetables and fruit. I have plenty of firewood. I can still make my way to the church on Sunday, where I pray for all the poor souls who have less than I do."

All Annie could do was nod. A plate was set in front of her. Ham, sliced potatoes that had been warmed in a fry pan, and some pickled carrots. A feast. Annie looked at it, her eyes devouring the food as she tried to remember the last time she'd eaten.

Sophia smiled and nodded. "Eat, señora. I will not harm you in any way. I cannot say the same for my nephew. By the same token, I cannot help you if that is your next question."

Annie forgot about her table manners as she wolfed down her food. It tasted better than any food she'd ever eaten in a five-star restaurant.

"Where did Rico go?" Annie asked when she cleaned her plate and pushed it to the middle of the plank table.

Enrico Araceli made his way to the village church. Sometimes, and he admitted to himself that those times were rare, he needed to communicate with God. And during those times, he stacked the deck and tried to barter with the deity. He'd list his accomplishments and omit mentioning all the things he had done wrong. He always promised that he would go to confession, but he never followed through.

He liked walking into a small church. Small churches were comforting, as opposed to the big cathedrals with all their stained glass and gilt. He also liked the scent of a small church. Maybe it was a remembrance from his childhood, when he was forced to attend daily mass. He sniffed. Yes, candle wax, lemon oil, and just the faint scent of incense. The cathedral's scents were overpowering, and he would always get sneezing fits.

Enrico dropped to his knees and blessed himself. What to say? Should he explain what he was doing and why he was doing it? *Why bother?* he asked himself. If it was true that God was all-knowing, then He knew what Enrico was doing and why he was doing it. He mumbled a childhood prayer for the souls of his mother and his uncle Armand.

Enrico slid back into the shiny pew, sliding a hymn book away from him. He looked around. The church was empty. It was quiet and peaceful. In his world of turmoil and angst, the feeling was alien. He closed his eyes and let his memories take over. He hated when he did this, but from time to time he tortured himself by allowing it to happen.

It was the eve of his sixteenth birthday. He was glued to the window, watching for his uncle Armand to arrive. His uncle had promised he'd be back for Enrico's birthday, but it was getting late. He wanted to cry, but sixteen-year-old boys didn't cry. Or, if they did, they did it in private, so no one would see. Maybe he would get here in the morning. Surely, his uncle wouldn't miss this momentous day.

Enrico whirled around, thinking his brothers were invading his privacy, but it wasn't

Mateo or Flavio; it was his mother. His eyes almost popped out of his head at the way she was dressed and painted up. Surely, she wasn't going out when Uncle Armand was due. But he knew that she was. He could smell her perfume all the way across the room. But what he hated even more was the smell on her when she returned. Usually early in the morning, when it was still dark outside.

"I came to say good night, Rico. You'll be asleep when I return. Tomorrow is your birthday. Tomorrow you become a man! Such a wonderful day."

Enrico drank in his mother's beauty. In his thoughts, he didn't know what to compare her to, so he simply thought of her as a princess queen. To him that said it all. When she smiled, she looked like an angel. At least to his young mind she was.

"Cook has your dinner on the table, Rico. Wash up; your brothers are already at the table. Run along now."

Run along. Like he was a little boy, like his brothers. He turned back to look out the window.

"Rico, sweetie, your dinner is waiting. Armand promised that he would be here for your birthday, and a promise is a promise."

"You're lying. If he is coming, then why are you going out all dressed up? He's not coming, and you know it."

"Rico, that is so harsh. How can you speak to me like that? What has gotten into you?"

"You! You're what's gotten into me. Where are you going? Why are you dressed up like a streetwalker? Where did you get those clothes anyway? I hate when you dress up like this. I really hate all that mess you put on your face."

"I'm going to a dinner party. I can't cancel now, it's too late. This is how you dress for an adult dinner party."

"No, it isn't, Mother. Stop trying to fool me. I'm sick of it. If Uncle Armand does get here, I'm going to tell him what you do and how you look when he isn't here," Enrico spat.

His mother's eyes narrowed. "Do that, my son, and you will regret the day you were born."

Enrico ignored her as he brushed past her and ran out to the kitchen. He hoped his mother would follow him, but he knew she wouldn't. He strained to hear the front door close. His shoulders slumped when he finally heard the sound he dreaded. His tears in check, he took his place at the table and started to eat the dinner he didn't want.

His younger brothers looked at him and made ugly faces, hoping to antagonize him, but he ignored them. He hated them and wasn't sure how he could hate his very own brothers. He had asked Armand that very question, and his uncle had stared at him for a long time before he answered him. And when he did, it wasn't a satisfactory answer. It's normal for children to hate one another one day and love them the next day. It was such a stupid response from a man whom he loved and adored. Because he could not remember a single time or day when he had loved his brothers.

His plate clean, Rico stared at his brothers before he left the table. He made his way back to the room they called the library to take up his position at the window. He pulled up short when he noticed his aunt Sophia staring out the same window. He could feel his eyes start to burn. He ran to her and didn't care if the tears trickled down his cheeks. He relished the feel of his aunt's arms circled around him. She crooned to him. He melted against her. "I told her I knew where she was going. I told her I was going to tell Uncle Armand. She said if I did, I would regret it."

"Shhh, it will be all right. Your uncle will be here soon. He called while you were eating your dinner. He said there was a terrible accident on the highway. He's coming, Rico, and he'll be here soon."

"And we will all lie as to where my mother is when he asks. Like we always do." Sophia nodded sadly as she hugged the young boy tighter. "Why do we do it, Aunt Sophia?"

"I wish I had the answer, but I don't. I guess the answer might be we're family, and family sticks together no matter what. Sadly, that doesn't make it right. Come, let's take a walk around the grounds to help clear our heads."

Hours later, Enrico felt a light tap on his shoulder. He rolled over to see his uncle Armand smiling down at him. *"Feliz cumpleaños,*

Rico. It's after midnight, so it is officially your birthday!"

Enrico bounded out of bed and hugged his uncle. "I waited all evening for you. I'm so glad to see you."

"I know, I know. Sophia told me. I'm sorry I'm so late. How about if we go down to the kitchen and I make us some hot chocolate with marshmallows. Should we wake your mother to join us?"

Enrico froze in place. "What time is it, Uncle?"

"A little after three. I hate to wake her up, though."

"No. No, we shouldn't wake her. She says she needs her beauty sleep." Enrico hoped his voice sounded as grown-up as he meant it to. It worked because Armand nodded and tossed the robe at the foot of the bed to him.

Uncle and nephew spent the next several hours drinking hot chocolate and talking about the latest soccer game, which Armand had attended. When the clock chimed five times in the hallway, Enrico felt a wave of fear engulf him. This was the hour his mother usually returned home, smelling her ugly smell. He bounded off his chair, pulling at his uncle's arm to get him to follow him. Upstairs, he made sure his uncle was secure in his room at the far end of the hall before he entered his own room, where he stood watch at the window once again, this time to watch for his mother's return.

He didn't know how he knew, but he knew that if his uncle saw and smelled his mother,

he would leave the house and never return.
He felt it in every pore of his body.

Enrico Araceli jerked upright when he heard
a loud banging behind him. The janitor with his
scrub bucket. Enrico got up, made the sign of
the cross, went down on one knee, then walked
down the aisle to where a bank of candles
waited. He struck a long match, lit a tall candle
that smelled like vanilla. He dropped several
euros into the slot and walked away.

As he walked down the wide center aisle he
realized he felt worse now than when he'd entered the church.

Sophia tilted her head to the side and said,
"Wherever he went, he's back. I hear his truck.
A word of caution, señora, do not antagonize
him."

The words were barely out of Sophia's mouth
when Rico burst through the door, his eyes full
of fire. He looked at the table, at Annie's empty
plate, then at his aunt. "I didn't tell you to feed
her; I told you to give her coffee."

A tirade in rapid-fire Spanish ensued, making it hard for Annie to follow what nephew
and aunt were saying to each other. Whatever
they were saying, Sophia was coming out on
the short end of the stick. Annie tensed just as
Enrico grabbed Sophia by her hair and literally tossed her across the room. Annie was off
the bench like she'd been shot from a cannon.

She lashed out, wishing she'd fared better with Harry Wong's martial arts lessons. She screamed at him about hitting a woman, a woman who had changed his diapers, as she pummeled him with her fists, but within seconds, he had her pinned against the table. He gave her a vicious punch to the stomach that brought her to her knees. Out of the corner of her eye, she could see Sophia wiping the blood off her forehead. Her eyes looked glazed as she tried to sit up.

"No more bullshit, eh. You Americans like that word, I am told. He grabbed Annie by the arm and slammed her down on the bench. Annie struggled to get her breath. Suddenly, Sophia was sitting across from her, a look of pure terror on her face.

"Now, I am going to ask you this only once, so think very carefully about your answer, Countess. What are these?" Annie tried to focus on the two special phones, hers and Myra's, and the two special gold shields. "Where did you get these, and what do they mean?"

"They were given to me and Myra. You're supposed to be so smart, figure it out."

"By whom?"

Annie could see no point in lying at this point. She risked a glance at Sophia, who seemed to be recovering and was paying attention to their dialogue. "The shields were given to Myra and me by the President of the United States. The phones were given to us by a man named Avery Snowden, who retired from Her Majesty's Secret Service."

"Why?" Enrico thundered.

A devil perched itself on Annie's shoulder. "Because I'm a spy! And so is my friend Myra, who escaped your clutches. Tools of the trade."

The blow when it came to Annie's cheekbone rocked her sideways. She could feel the warm trickle of blood running down her cheek. "What, you can't handle the truth?" Mentally she flipped the pages of Kathryn's playbook till she found one she liked.

"You're a wuss, a man who beats on women, a bastard whose mother was a slut. You're a nothing! The moment Myra makes contact with our people, and she will, you can take that to the bank, they will be here in such droves you won't know what hit you. One of our people is an expert with a knife. Your manhood will be just a memory when she's done with you. You can take that one to the bank, too. Oh, and once she slices it off, she'll shove it up your tight ass."

"You're lying!" Enrico screamed. "What kind of spies are two old women?"

"We work for the CIA during the week; then they lend us out to the FBI for weekends. Two elderly ladies raise no suspicion."

"You're lying!" Enrico barked a second time.

Annie sighed. "No, Enrico, I am not lying."

"Call your bankers right now. Tell them to make arrangements to pay my brothers and me my father's share of the estate. If you don't, my men in the village will start to kill all the villagers. Here," Enrico said, shoving one of the special phones across the table to Annie. "When you tell them that, they will do as you say. If they don't, the deaths of the villagers will be on you. Make sure you convey that to your financial people. After you do that, you will write out a release that I can have published to the courts saying that I am the son of Count Armand de Silva."

"Well, sure, Enrico. I can do that. Nothing like advertising to the whole world that you and your brothers are illegitimate. I personally don't think anyone cares even a little bit."

It wasn't a blow this time, it was a mighty shove that sent Annie backward and off the bench. She landed with a painful thud, stunned. A searing pain ran down her arm. A broken bone, a dislocated shoulder? She bit down on her lower lip, trying to cope. She could hear Sophia start to screech at her nephew. Once again, the tirade was so quick and fast she could only make out a few words here and there. Did Sophia really call him a maggot on a pig's ass? Evidently so, because suddenly Sophia was lying next to her, moaning and crying.

"Stupid women!" Enrico raged.

"Sophia is right, you're worse than a maggot on a pig's ass!" Annie shot back.

Enrico hauled Annie to her feet and slammed her down on the bench. "Make the call. And you had best be convincing, Countess."

Annie tried to fight the pain in her arm as she pressed the digits on the phone that would connect her to Connor, her chief financial officer. When she heard his voice, she went into her spiel. "Connor, I want you to listen to me very carefully. You are to release half of all my holdings to Armand's illegitimate son, who is standing over me to make sure I tell you what he will do if you don't follow orders. He and his thugs are holding an entire village captive, and he is threatening to kill the villagers one by one unless you do as he says. Connor, there are women and children in the village and two priests. Break the rules, do whatever you have to do. Call Charles Martin and tell him what I just told you as he is second-in-command as you well know. Tell me you understand everything I just said to you, because my captor is standing over me listening to this conversation. You are to expedite this, Connor."

The voice on the other end of the phone sounded scratchy and tinny. "I'll call a special meeting immediately. Save me some time and give me Martin's phone number."

Annie looked at Enrico, her eyes full of hate. She rattled off Charles's phone number.

Enrico snatched the phone away and stared at Annie, who looked him right in the eye and didn't flinch. "I don't think he believed you, Countess."

"When it comes to life and death, my people will do what they have to do. They are not barbarians like you and your brothers."

Enrico snorted. "You could have saved yourself months of captivity and pain by doing this the first time I asked you. You forced me into this position."

Annie said nothing. She tried to focus and

get past the pain in her arm. She watched as Enrico gathered up the phones and the gold shields to put in a small burlap sack he pulled out of his pocket. He held up one of the gold shields. "This may surprise you, but I know what this is. I have a friend in a very high place who told me about a directive his office received years ago concerning these special shields. The bearer gets, how do you Americans say, a free ride. Nothing will happen to me as long as I have these shields.

"I have a few matters to attend to. I'll be back before dark, so be prepared, Countess, to finish your journey. I'm going to tie you up now, and my men will watch over you till I get back."

Enrico turned then to his aunt. "As for you, Auntie Sophia, I will deal with you on my return. Feed my men after I leave; they've had nothing to eat today."

Sophia let loose with another string of obscenities that sounded worse than the other two times she went off on her nephew. He laughed at her as he yanked at the rope he was using to tie Annie to the leg of the plank table.

Annie cursed under her breath, all of Kathryn's favorite swearwords, and a few of her own thrown into the mix.

Enrico continued to laugh, an ugly, obscene sound, as he stomped from the house. He slammed the door so hard that the glass rattled.

Sophia moved then, faster than Annie

thought possible. She started to babble half in Spanish and half in English just as the three guards from outside entered the house and took a seat at the table, at which point Sophia switched to just English. "They do not understand English," she said as she banged pots and pans in preparation to feeding Enrico's thugs. "I have a plan," she hissed.

"I'm glad somebody does," Annie mumbled as she watched Sophia slice ham. She almost missed Sophia's sleight-of-hand movement when she snipped bits of green leaves from a plant on the windowsill.

One of the thugs sitting at the table stretched out his legs and kicked Annie in the knee. She yelped in pain. Sophia whirled around and cursed at the men, who just laughed at her. She leaned over Annie, and whispered, "I have changed my mind. I am going to help you." Annie swooned as she tried to suck up the pain that was rapidly invading her body.

Back at the stove, Sophia filled three plates with sliced potatoes and the same pickled carrots from a large crock on the kitchen counter that she had served Annie earlier, but these carrots were sprinkled with bits of greenery as a garnish. The final thing she added to the plates was the last of the ham. Annie watched as the men dived into the food like they hadn't eaten in days.

Annie never took her eyes off the men. She waited.

Sophia waited.

Annie started to count down in her head. Ten minutes later, she wanted to raise her fist in victory, but her hands were tied. One by one, the three men toppled over to land on the floor. Sophia gave each of them a solid kick to his head before she untied Annie. She handed Annie a handful of aspirin and some water. "It's all I have. It might help a little with the pain. Can you walk?"

"If I have to. Did you kill them? I don't care if you did, I just want to know."

"No. But when they wake up, hours from now, they will feel like they're dead. Enrico will be furious. Hurry now, you have to leave here. I have a moped out back, and it has enough gas in it to get you to town. I'll draw you a map, so you can take secondary roads to avoid running into Enrico if he comes back early. Go to your embassy, where you will be safe. Are you really a spy? Is what you told my nephew true?"

Annie wanted to laugh, but her head hurt too much. "I am, and yes, it's all true. You can't stay here; you have to come with me."

"No, I can't go with you. I have a bicycle. I'll go somewhere safe."

"Oh, no. No, no, you are coming with me. Enrico will find you, and he *will* kill you. The man is insane. You know it as well as I do. You do not deserve this. My people will protect you, Sophia. Truly they will. I saw people on the road riding double on the mopeds. Show me where the moped is, and let's get out of here. Are you sure they aren't dead?"

"I'm sure, señora. Very well, you speak the truth. I am not ready to go to meet my Maker. Not yet. I will go with you. I will drive the moped, but you will have to hold on to me very tightly. The roads are bad."

"I can do that." Annie wondered if what she said was true since she could barely move her arm. It was all she could do not to let go and black out with the pain in her shoulder and arm.

Sophia opened the door, looked out both ways, and motioned for Annie to follow her. Annie struggled to her feet, then stood over the three thugs. She bent over to search the men's pockets. She tossed the cell phones to the side, then looked for the wallets. She took all their money, handing it to Sophia, who didn't demur. Annie looked at the leader of the trio, the one with the gun. Should she take it or not? Hell yes, Kathryn would have said. Annie picked up the gun and hefted it, to feel the balance.

Sophia gasped and blessed herself as she backed away, her eyes wide. "Do . . . Do you know how . . . to shoot a gun, señora?" she asked fearfully.

"I'm a crack shot. Annie Oakley the second." Annie grinned.

"What is that . . . crack shot?"

"That means whatever I aim at, I hit, center mass. Now my friend Myra, the one who got away from your nephew, can't shoot worth a darn. If she was standing in front of a barn door and pulled the trigger, she'd somehow manage to hit a tree."

In spite of herself, Sophia laughed. Annie thought it was a youthful sound, a happy sound, and yet she knew that Sophia didn't have much in her life to make her laugh.

"I need something to carry all this in. Do you have a sack of some kind?"

Sophia scurried back into the kitchen and rummaged under the sink. She pulled out a black nylon bag with a Nike logo on it. "Flavio, Rico's brother, left this here a long time ago. Hurry, señora, we need to leave here."

Annie dumped the cell phones into the bag, along with the gun. She spent a few minutes staring down at the three thugs. One by one she stomped on their noses. She threw her good arm in the air when she saw blood spurt in every direction. *Myra, you would be so proud of me right now.*

Annie followed Sophia around to the back of the little house, where there was a small toolshed. She noticed the dying garden, the flower beds that were now dormant. It was obvious that Sophia liked digging in the rich, loamy soil. She just knew she raised a bumper crop of vegetables. She wondered if the little lady cut the flowers and filled her house with them when they bloomed.

Sophia backed up the moped and turned it toward the front of the house. She settled herself on the padded seat, then slung the Nike bag over the handlebars. Annie slid on the back end of the seat and wrapped her good arm around Sophia's waist. "Go!"

Sophia was right, the roads were terrible, potholes the size of dinner plates all over the place. Sophia did her best to avoid them, weaving in and out and around. Annie thanked God there was little to no traffic on the country road.

Twenty minutes into the kidney-crushing ride, Sophia slowed the moped and pulled to the side of the road. She pointed to the Nike bag. "All the phones are ringing! Now, mine is ringing," Sophia said as she pulled her own cell phone out of her pocket. "What do you want me to do, señora?"

Annie shrugged. She was saved from a reply when the phones stopped ringing, even Sophia's.

"Rico will figure it out. Right now, he's probably halfway to the Village of Tears. I think he will call on more people like those we left behind, and they will be here soon. We need to stick to the back roads. I'm thinking that he will have his people staked out at your consulate. Tell me what you want to do, señora."

"I need to call my people. How can I call out of the country?"

"You can't do that with these phones. They are in-country only. The cheapest version sold on the market. Think about it, why would we need to call out of the country?"

Annie's hopes crashed. "Okay, okay. Do you know where there is an Internet café?"

"No, I don't. I never had a reason to use an Internet café. I am sure there are many of them in the heart of town. But first, señora, I am taking you to a doctor I know. I do not like how pale you look. And I think you might have a concussion. You need to be in good condition to continue on."

Annie didn't give a second thought to protesting. She didn't know how much longer she could stand the pain in her shoulder and arm. She simply nodded.

Thirty minutes later, Sophia steered the moped onto a tree-lined street with pleasant-looking cottages on both sides. She drove to the end of the street and up onto a gravel driveway.

Sophia tapped the small horn on the moped. A moment later the door opened, and a wizened old man stepped onto the stoop. He peered at his unexpected guests and smiled when he recognized Sophia.

"I brought you a patient who needs your help. Your *discreet* help. Can you help us?"

"For you, my dear Sophia, the answer is yes. Do you need to secure your moped?"

"Yes, that would be . . . helpful. First, though, see to my friend. Señora, can you walk on your own?"

"Of course," Annie said as she tottered forward on shaky legs.

"Go, then, while I take our transportation around to the back of the house."

"The bag, Sophia."

"I will not let it out of my sight, señora. Go now."

Annie made it up the walkway, across a patch of dry grass, and up the three steps to where the doctor waited before her legs buckled. The old doctor caught her just in time.

"Relax, señora, you are in good hands now. Safe hands."

The last thing Annie remembered before she passed out were the words *safe hands*.

Chapter 9

Annie woke and knew instantly where she was and how she'd gotten there. The room wasn't totally dark. She could see a faint yellowish glow from a lamp at the far end of the room. It gave off just enough light for her to see Sophia curled into a ball on a chair next to her bed.

It took Annie a few minutes to realize that the burning, knifelike pain in her shoulder and arm was gone, leaving only a dull ache to contend with. She let her gaze rake the room for a sign of a clock, but there was no clock that she could see. Her treasured oversize Mickey Mouse watch was gone, thanks to Enrico Araceli. She wondered what he would do with it. *Evil bastard,* she thought.

Annie stared at Sophia. She was so glad that Sophia had stepped up to the plate and helped her. For that she would be forever grateful. God alone knew where she would be without the little woman's help.

Sophia stirred, then opened her eyes. "Señora, are you all right?"

"Yes. Did I wake you?" What a silly question. She'd made no noise.

"I was just dozing. How do you feel?"

Annie pondered the question. "Overall, much better; the terrible pain is gone, but my arm aches. My knee is throbbing. How long did I sleep?"

"It's almost dawn. The doctor set your shoulder. He had to put it back in the socket. He said you would ache. He will drain the fluid on your knee later this morning. He is a very good doctor, señora."

"How do you know him? Is he your physician?"

"Yes and no. He took care of my sister. She used to flirt outrageously with him. He never responded. This might surprise you, but he is only sixty-three years old. He has a medical condition that ages him prematurely. His practice is limited these days."

Annie was wide-awake now. "I am so grateful to you, Sophia. I don't know how to thank you. When this is all over and done with, I'd like to take you to America with me. I know people who can arrange this. I can set you up in a house like the one Armand bought for you that will be truly yours. You can paint all day long. You can garden and grow your flowers and join a church of your choosing. I make this offer to you because, as I said, when it's all over, you will have no one left here in the way of family. I'm willing to make you part of my immediate family, none of whom are blood relatives. Will you think about it?"

Sophia hesitated, then nodded.

"You didn't like your sister very much, did you?"

"No, in some ways I was jealous. She was the beautiful one. And she was truly beautiful. On the outside. That's what men like, I'm told. Inside, she was not pretty. She was mean, manipulative, and calculating. She wasn't a good mother, although, and I know that this will be hard for you to believe, Armand was a good father. I think he truly loved the children. I say this to you in all honesty, señora.

"I do not know if my sister truly loved Armand or not. My opinion is she did not. But she loved his title, all the material things he bestowed on her. I do not want to hurt you, but Armand was besotted with her. He loved her very much. Often, he would talk to me of her and his feelings. My heart breaks for you the way he deceived and betrayed you."

"I'm past that now. Tell me something. You never call your sister by name. You just say, my sister. Why is that? What was her name?"

Sophia got off the chair, rolled her shoulders to release the tension and stress from spending long hours curled into a ball on the chair, and approached Annie's bed. She reached down for Annie's hand and held it tight. "There was a reason for that, señora. I did not want to cause you pain. My sister's name was . . . it was . . . Elena."

Annie stiffened in the bed as her own hand squeezed Sophia's in return. It was such a blow, she almost blacked out.

"I know," Sophia whispered. "I know. I was so hoping that you would never ask."

"I wanted to name our daughter Angela Marie. Armand fought with me. It was the only time we ever argued. He was adamant that we name our daughter Maria Elena, and he said we would call her Elena because every other woman in Spain was named Maria. He finally wore me down, and I consented because I loved him. How could he have done that to me, Sophia? How?"

"The heart wants what the heart wants," Sophia said, sadness ringing in her voice.

Annie struggled with her thoughts. She had to let it go, no matter how painful it was. "Is there anything else you think I should know about my deceased husband?" she finally croaked in a harsh whisper.

Sophia squared her shoulders. "Isn't that enough, señora?"

"I think so, Sophia. And now that we're on such an intimate level, please call me Annie. I hate being called señora. Makes me feel old. Like *really* old."

Sophia chuckled. "Very well . . . Annie."

Annie gave herself a mental shake. "What's our game plan once your doctor drains the fluid from my knee? Oh, good Lord, does the doctor have a phone that will allow me to call out of the country? Does he have a computer?"

"I don't know. We can ask him when he comes in to check on you."

"If not, we have to find an Internet café."

"While you were sleeping, the doctor loaned me his car, and I rode to town. I wanted to check out the U.S. Consulate. I did not see anyone I knew. However, I did notice something that I thought was strange. There were men on the boulevard who looked like they didn't belong there. They were just walking aimlessly up and down. I watched for over an hour from a very good vantage point. What I noticed in particular was there was always one man near the gate. From time to time, they would speak to each other on their phones. There were a total of six. I think they are working for my nephew. I do not think I am wrong . . . Annie."

"Then to be on the safe side, we have to scratch the idea of going to the embassy. By any chance, did you search out an Internet café?"

"I did, but I also saw some people there who looked to me like they had no clue what an Internet café is. There was only one in the area. I think we would have to go to downtown, which is even farther, and try to find one that Rico can't send his thugs to watch. He simply cannot have that many people on his side doing his evil bidding. I'm thinking we might have to take the doctor into our confidence if you have no objection. He can be trusted, Annie. I am absolutely positive of this."

"Maybe the good doctor *can* help us. If you vouch for him, then I'm okay with confiding in him. If nothing else, it's a jumping-off spot. Let's not worry too much until we talk to him. I truly believe there is a solution to every problem. One just has to find it. Thank you for all your help. I realize you did not sign up for this, and for that I am truly sorry, Sophia."

Sophia just nodded and returned to the chair she'd been sleeping in. "It's starting to get light out. The doctor should be here soon. He once told me years ago that he does not sleep much. I think he stews and frets about his patients. He has never married and has no family. My sister told me that. I do not even think he has a housekeeper here. It would appear he takes care of himself and the few patients he sees to."

Annie did not miss the lilt in Sophia's voice when she spoke of the doctor. Aha, she thought. But wise woman that she was, Annie kept her thoughts to herself.

All conversation came to a halt when a knock sounded on the bedroom door. Sophia was off her chair as though she'd been shot from a cannon. She raced to the door and flung it open. Annie winced at how chipper her voice was, how welcoming.

"And how is our patient this morning, Sophia?" The tone of the doctor's voice matched Sophia's.

Well, well, what have we here? Annie mused.

Before Sophia could respond, she said, "I feel much better, Doctor, but my knee is throbbing quite a lot. I feel rested. Thank you for your help."

"That's what I'm here for. Sophia, the wheelchair is outside the door. Would you please fetch it, so I can take our patient to the examining room? And I do have a favor to ask of you."

Sophia's face lit up like a Roman candle. "Of course, anything."

"While I drain the fluid from our patient, would you consider making us some of those delicious pancakes you used to make for your sister and her boys? Everything you need is in the kitchen. And some bacon. Good coffee. Mine always tastes like dishwater. I used to dream about those breakfasts long after . . . Well, for months and months, after I was no longer on call for your family."

"Of course." Annie winked at Sophia, who became so flustered that she literally ran from the room. She gave the wheelchair a push at the door and it rolled across the floor, stopping right at the doctor's feet. And then she was gone.

An hour later, Annie hobbled behind the doctor down the hall and out to the kitchen, where delicious aromas welcomed them. The pressure from her swollen knee was gone. All she felt now was a dull ache that she was very hopeful would go away soon.

The doctor made sure that Annie was comfortably seated before he motioned for Sophia to join them. "All right, ladies, let's talk turkey!" he said sternly. "Isn't that what you Americans say when you are about to speak of something that is deadly serious?

"Do not think for one minute that either one of you fooled me with that ridiculously silly story on your arrival to account for our patient's condition. *TALK!*" he boomed.

Both women's words came faster than a runaway train, faster than flying bullets as they spoke over each other. They were shrill, subdued, and tearful as they talked over each other in order to get everything out into the open as quickly as possible. Somehow or other, perhaps from years of listening to distraught patients pouring out their stories, the doctor managed to make sense of it all. He nodded, rubbed at his freshly shaved chin, and then signaled to indicate that Sophia could get on with the pancakes.

Annie took a deep breath. "I need your help. Actually, Sophia and I both need your help. I don't trust Enrico not to return to harm her once he finds out she helped me escape."

"Yes, yes, yes, I understand. Tell me what you want me to do. I have no patients today. I am at your complete disposal."

"First things first. Are we safe here, Doctor?"

"Yes, Enrico forgot about me months ago. Since we're going to be partners here, I suggest we go with first names. You may call me Andres. My full name is Andres Miguel. Dr. Andres Miguel. I am an internist with a nonexistent practice. By my own choice," he added hastily.

"I suppose I should explain that. I have a rare medical condition that required that I curtail my practice. I couldn't afford all the equipment I would need to treat patients. I wish I could have X-rayed your knee to be certain a bone wasn't chipped. Back when I was practicing medicine full time, I would have sold my life away for an MRI machine. A CAT scan machine. But even then, I still couldn't afford those costly machines. I'm just a simple country doctor these days. I can't even afford a nurse or a day lady. My fees are mostly paid in produce or chickens. All right, enough of me. I think we should now avail ourselves of those delicious-looking pancakes. We can talk again when we finish eating."

Annie smiled, thinking about Charles's rule of not discussing business while eating. She didn't feel particularly hungry but surprised herself by cleaning her plate and drinking two cups of coffee.

As she chewed, she let her mind wander. She liked the good doctor. More important, she trusted him. God was indeed smiling on her by leading her first to Sophia, then to the doctor.

Andres surprised both Annie and Sophia when he said, "I'll clean up since Sophia cooked. Annie is a patient and a guest, so she doesn't enter into the equation." He bent over and kissed Sophia on the cheek. "It was a wonderful breakfast, Sophia, just the way I remembered. I can multitask, ladies, so we can talk."

Sophia's face turned beet red. Annie grinned and looked away.

"Do you have a computer, Andres?"

"I did, but it died on me a few years ago. I couldn't afford to replace it."

"I assume you have a phone. Can I call out of the country on it?"

"No, it's just your basic phone. However, I can ride into town and go to the Internet café that Sophia checked out. I think I can handle that. I'm known in town. People might wonder what I'm doing in a place like that, but I don't think they'll talk among themselves. If I act like I belong, in case someone is watching the café, I'll just be a local availing myself of the café's computers. I'll keep my eyes and ears open. Tell me what you want me to do."

"I'll write down the e-mail addresses and the phone numbers in case you can send texts. I'm sure someone in the café will be able to help you with that. I'll need a pencil and paper."

Andres dried his hands on a pristine hand towel before he rummaged in a drawer for paper and pencil. He handed them over.

Annie carefully wrote down everyone's e-mail, then wrote out a short script for Andres to follow. You will have to wait for a response to the e-mails. If you don't hear back within twenty minutes, try texting the numbers I listed. Your keyword is 'Annie' on the subject line.

"I don't know for sure if my people are here or not. Enough time has gone by for them to have made the trip. Tell them to come and get me. You know my full story, so if they question you, you know how to respond. Are you sure you can do this, Andres?"

"I can do this. When you see me next, I hope to have good news for you. In the meantime, stay off your leg for the next few hours. Keep it propped up the way you have it now. Are you sure you don't want any pain pills?"

"I'm sure. But I will take a few aspirin. Good luck, Andres."

Andres wiggled his eyebrows. "This is the most excitement I've had in years. Behave yourselves, ladies, until I return.

"It looks to be a nice day, but rain is expected soon. Sit in the wheelchair and go outdoors and get some fresh air. Sophia, make fresh coffee, please. I'll be back as soon as I can. Oh, give me your phone number so I can call you if I run into problems."

Sophia left the room and returned with the black Nike duffel. She dumped the contents on the kitchen table. If Andres was surprised to see the gun, he didn't show it.

Sophia pawed through the phones until she found the one that was hers. She turned it on. "I didn't bring the charger, but I still have two bars." She rattled off the number. Andres copied it onto the paper Annie had handed over.

Andres waved airily. Minutes later, they heard the engine of his car come to life.

"He's a nice man. Thank you for bringing me here, Sophia."

"Yes, he is a nice man. He cares about people."

* * *

Andres Miguel liked going into town. Not that he did it often, but sometimes on the weekends, he would treat himself to a Sunday morning breakfast at an outdoor café. Invariably, people who had known him and been treated by him years earlier before he'd retired to the country would stop by. He loved the short meetings and playing what he called catch-ups. It was also a good time to read his medical journals, so he could keep up with the latest medical news. Sometimes, he would even allow himself to feel sorry about the path his life had taken, but those feelings never lasted long.

He loved this town, or as he thought of it, the village of thirty thousand inhabitants. It was modern and up to date. But at the end of the day, he was always glad to get back to his little gabled house in the country. He thought then about Sophia and how he'd felt when he opened the door to see her standing there with her strange friend, whom he had liked instantly. He remembered how his heart had skipped a beat and how his ears and neck turned warm. He made a mental note to himself to think about that, but later. Now he had a mission, and he did not want to disappoint the ladies.

Andres drove cautiously. He did everything cautiously, more so these days than when he was younger. Something else he needed to think about later on.

Andres searched for a parking space and almost laughed out loud when he saw an elderly gentleman pull away from the curb just two buildings down from the Internet café. He knew this area well because of the pharmacy and the café where he used to go on Sunday mornings.

Mindful of Sophia's report that there were men on the boulevard who looked like they didn't belong, Andres decided he needed to do some reconnaissance. He laughed silently as he envisioned himself as some sort of super-spy. He walked up to the pharmacy and looked at the window display. Cosmetics on one side. He closed his eyes and sniffed. Even through the glass, he could smell the perfumes and powders. He liked the smell. It brought back a memory of his many house calls to Elena Araceli's bedroom, which had contained more cosmetics and perfumes than the pharmacy's show window.

He shook his head to clear his thoughts. He was here to spy, so he needed to start spying. He stared into the glass to see which people were walking by and who was loitering. He spotted two men dressed in jeans and T-shirts, baggy shirts, big enough to hide a gun if it was tucked into the back of the men's jeans. Maybe he had the makings of a supersleuth after all. The thought pleased him for some reason.

Andres moved to the other side of the pharmacy door to look at a display of vitamins. He moved on, past a hardware store featuring battery-driven wheelbarrows, and then to the Internet café. He carried a folder with several other folders tucked inside. Something had told him to take it when he left the house, and he'd just grabbed it. Part of his MO. He grinned to himself. He was playing a part, and he loved it.

Just as his hand reached the handle on the door, one of the men he'd seen in the plate-glass window of the pharmacy came up to him. Andres tried to push at the door, but the man stuck out his arm. "Why are you here?"

"What? Why are you asking me that? It's none of your business why I'm here. Move, young man."

The man didn't move. "Do I have to call the police?" Andres asked.

The man finally stepped aside, and Andres walked inside. The first person he saw was the man's double, standing near the counter, where customers signed up for computer use. Andres felt his heart start to beat faster. He approached the young girl behind the counter and smiled. "Stephanie!"

The girl was perhaps fifteen or so, and he'd delivered her at her birth, then saw to all her medical needs for years until he'd moved to the country. "How is your family?" he asked in Spanish.

"Dr. Miguel! How nice to see you! Papa had a dental appointment. Mama has the early shift at the hospital, and since I'm on Christmas break from school, I'm working here until he gets back. Don't frown at me." She giggled. "What can I do for you today?"

Knowing the man outside was listening, Andres continued with his role-playing. "My computer at home died on me, and I need to input some patient information onto a flash drive. I need an hour, possibly an hour and a half." He withdrew a credit card with a zero balance that he hadn't used in several years and had no way of knowing if it was still good or not.

Stephanie ran the card, then pulled a paper out of the machine for him to sign his name. Out of the corner of his eye, he watched as the man whose arms were so tattooed that no sign of his actual flesh could be seen glared at him. He glared right back. He felt relieved as Stephanie led the way to a computer and explained what he had to do.

It took Andres exactly ten minutes to set up a Yahoo e-mail account, and another fifteen minutes to type out e-mail messages to all the names on Annie's list. "Do you have an international phone here, Stephanie?" he whispered. The young girl nodded. "I might have to make a call. How do I do that? I don't want that man overhearing or knowing what I'm doing. Why is he here? Who is he, do you know?"

Stephanie shook her head. "I don't know who he is. He said he's waiting for someone. He's been here since I opened the café at nine o'clock. He's already had four cups of coffee. I can bring you the phone. I won't run the charge until you make the call. I can be discreet," she said, giggling. Andres nodded as he focused on the computer screen in front of him. He looked up at a bank of wall clocks that told the time all over the world. At first he was puzzled; then he realized that most people were probably communicating with people in other parts of the world, so seeing what time it was in other places was a good thing.

Time crawled by, minute by minute. Andres started to itch. Maybe the e-mails didn't go through. Maybe the recipients didn't recognize the e-mail address and deleted them. Maybe he should resend them or, better yet, open up another Yahoo e-mail account in Anna de Silva's name. Yes, yes, that was what he would do. Leave no stone unturned. He knew he wouldn't be able to bear the looks of disappointment on Sophia's and Annie's faces if he returned a failure.

Now that he more or less knew what he was doing, Andres quickly set up a new account in Annie's name. He had just finished the first e-mail to someone named Charles Martin when he became aware of a commotion in front of the café. A lady who could have posed as a double for Anna de Silva was arguing with the tattooed man he'd exchanged glaring looks with. Stephanie was calling the woman by name, Mrs. Simone, and telling the man to leave her alone or she would call the police. The man ignored her threat as Mrs. Simone cursed and screeched as she tried to lash out at the man. Andres watched as one of the customers jumped up from his station to rush to the woman's aid. He saw it all in slow motion as Stephanie pressed the 112 digits on the phone in her hand. He had to do something

and do it *now*. He ran forward to help the customer just as two men from outside rushed in
to help their partner, guns in their hands.

"Stop! Or I will shoot you!"

There were no fools in the café. Everyone
froze in place, except Mrs. Simone, who continued to screech and curse. And then they all
heard the unmistakable sounds of the police
sirens, known and understood all over the
world; then a heartbeat later, flashing blue
lights could be seen as the sirens continued
their wail. Right behind the two police cars another vehicle, a news van, pulled alongside.
Reporters and cameramen spilled out onto
the sidewalk as everyone rushed to enter the
café, where Mrs. Simone was screeching about
how all she wanted to do was engage with her
family on Facebook and how these thugs wres-
tled her to the ground to try to steal the
printed-out e-mails in her purse.

It took Andres all of three seconds to realize
he was on camera. His heart almost beat itself
out of his chest. He turned, looked at Stephanie,
and asked for the phone. Never taking her eyes
off what was going on in front of her, as she wondered how she was going to explain to her father how this had happened on her watch, she
handed it over.

Andres scurried back to his station. No return e-mails. He followed the instructions and
dialed the cell numbers Annie had written out.
As he waited for a connection, he kept his eyes
glued to what was going on in the main part of
the café. When he heard a voice on the other end

of the phone, he lost his memory. He couldn't remember whose number he had called. He started
to babble, starting off with, "I can only repeat
this once since we are under siege at this location, so listen to me . . ." When he read off the
entire script Annie had written out for him, he
was physically exhausted. He sat down and did
his best to get his breathing back under control. He had to act normal—and he needed to
get out of there. But that didn't look like it was
going to happen anytime soon. What to do?
Call Sophia. Alert her and Annie.

The tattooed twins, along with another one
of their crew, were in custody, he was happy to
see that. Mrs. Simone had finally shut up and
was crying softly, with Stephanie's arms around
her shoulder. She kept repeating over and over,
"They think I'm someone else. They were going
to kidnap me, and my family would never see
me again."

Then she started to screech and curse again.
Andres wanted to put his fingers in his ears.

One of the officers, a young man whose patience was wearing thin, gave a sharp whistle
for silence. Even Mrs. Simone clamped her lips
shut.

"Now, one at a time, tell me what happened
here. You are all safe now, as you can see. Those
three men are in our custody and will be dealt
with. We need to take all your statements."

Andres stepped forward. He identified himself. Stephanie vouched for him, but he held
out his driver's license and his small medical
card encased in plastic. "When I first got here,

I noticed the man who came in from outside. There were two others who appeared to be with him. I assume they fled. I just want you to know there were more men." All the while, he knew he was being recorded. He hoped and prayed that Enrico Araceli and his two brothers were not watching the noonday news or what they called Breaking News ahead of the regular newscast. He had to call Sophia. He looked at the officer, whose patience was being tried, and asked rather timidly if he could call his office to let them know he would be late. The police officer shook his head. No meant no. Andres sat down at his workstation, his heart jumping all over the place. He risked a glance at the computer screen. No return messages.

Bottom line. He'd failed. Unless . . . the person who answered his phone call acted on the message. He'd tried. There was nothing more he could do. Well, that wasn't quite true. There was one more thing he could do. Pray. So he prayed. Fervently.

Chapter 10

Sophia held the door leading to the doctor's outdoor patio so Annie could limp her way through. She waited for Annie to settle herself in one of the wicker chairs before she returned to the kitchen to fetch two cups of fresh coffee. No sooner had she settled herself when she felt the first raindrops splatter on the round glass table.

"Oh, dear, this was a mistake. Come, Annie! It's starting to rain. We can watch television until the doctor gets back. Besides, it's chilly out here, and we'll be more comfortable indoors."

Annie heaved her shivering body out of the wicker chair and followed Sophia indoors. Once again, she settled herself and propped up her leg. She realized it had stopped aching. Such a welcome relief to realize she was virtually pain-free for the moment. She made a mental note never to take anything for granted again.

Sophia started to giggle. "This television set is so small, we might go blind trying to watch anything on it. The good news is we can hear what's going on. I like to keep up with what's going on locally. We have here what we call midmorning news during the week. Enrico is obsessed with it. No matter where he is or what he does, he stops and listens on his phone. I don't understand how that all works, but I guess he does. First they do the weather, though. Sometimes they actually get it right. Like now."

Annie half listened to Sophia and the sharp-sounding voice coming from the tiny television set on the counter. She was worried, so much so that she couldn't concentrate on anything but Myra and the Sisters. Were they looking for her? More to the point, would they find her? Had the doctor been successful in contacting Charles and Avery? Her stomach tied itself into a knot as her thoughts took her to dark places where she didn't even hear what the local newscaster was saying.

Annie did her best to come out of the dark space she was stuck in when she heard Sophia scream, "Come! Come! Hurry, Annie!"

"What? What's wrong? What's wrong, Sophia?"

Sophia pointed to the tiny television. She turned up the volume as high as it would go. Annie shook her head to clear her thoughts as she squinted to see the tiny figures on the screen. She immediately recognized Dr. Miguel. She knew how to put two and two together. Enrico was going to see this newscast since he was obsessed with the midmorning news. He would probably be faster at putting two and two together than she was. He would recognize Dr. Miguel and realize this was where Sophia had brought her. He would either be on his way, or he would have people coming here.

"My nephew is very smart, Annie. He will come here. Trust me. We must leave here and make sure there is no trace of our having been here. Do what you can here in the kitchen to erase our presence. I will make up the beds and see to the surgery room. I think the doctor can handle the fallout on his return. Hurry now, we don't have much time, and we will be fighting bad weather. See if you can find some rain gear."

Annie moved then as fast as her game leg allowed. She put away all of the dishes and hung up the damp dishtowel. Yes, the kitchen smelled like food, but the doctor had to eat. She pushed the chairs back under the table but left one at an angle, the doctor's chair if he was eating breakfast alone. She looked around. Neat and tidy, a bachelor's home.

Annie hobbled over to the kitchen closet by the back door. Heavy jackets, snow boots, rain gear, a yellow slicker, and a dark green poncho. She felt like she'd just won the lottery. Annie scooped them up and closed the door just as Sophia swooped into the room like some avenging bird. She looked around and nodded that she was satisfied with the job Annie had done.

Annie held out the rain gear. Sophia chose the yellow slicker as Annie pulled the green poncho over her head and settled it over her shoulders. No matter what, she was going to get wet. She shrugged.

"Come! Come!"

"Where are we going?"

"To the last place Enrico will think to look for us. His own apartment here in town."

In spite of herself, Annie laughed out loud. "I like the way you think. You're as devious as the Sisters. How far is it?"

"Forty minutes or so. Traffic, rainfall, police. Possibly more."

Annie ripped a page out of Kathryn's playbook and cursed long and loud. "My people will never be able to find us now."

"Do not be so sure. Dr. Miguel will figure it all out once he sees we're gone. I think he will go back to the Internet café and call your people again. I told you he is a very smart man. He'll think about places I might go, and eventually, he'll figure it out. Just in case he isn't as smart as I think he is, I left a clue for him."

"Oh, you dear sweet woman. I love you. What's the clue?" Annie asked as she settled herself behind Sophia on the moped.

"I left a drawing in the doctor's surgery. He keeps crayons and paper in there for children. I drew a stick drawing of a child and a dog and cat listening to the news. I signed it *Cissie*. I left it on the little desk he keeps in the corner.

He'll figure it out. Everyone who has ever come in contact with Enrico knows about his obsession with the news. No more talking now. I have to pay attention to the road, and it is difficult to see with all this rain coming down. Hold on to me as tight as you can. The wind is starting to whip up. This might be a good time to pray, Annie."

Annie did pray then, prayers she'd learned in her childhood that she to this day said every single day of her life. She didn't ask for anything. She couldn't bring herself to barter with God. The prayers in themselves were comforting, and that was all she needed for now. And her belief that God was on her side.

Andres Miguel climbed out of his car and ran to his house. He was about to shout out his success when he realized someone was standing in his kitchen drinking coffee out of one of his cups. He sucked in a deep breath. Play it cool, Andres warned himself. Slow and easy. "Enrico! What's wrong? Did something happen to your brothers? What are you doing here? Are you all right? It's been so long since we've seen each other." He stopped just short of babbling and looked Enrico in the eye. He tossed the manila folder on the table before he proceeded to pour himself a cup of coffee.

"Where are they?"

"Who?"

"Don't be coy, old man. I'm not in the mood. Now, where are they?"

Andres set his cup down on the table and looked at Enrico, hoping he looked as innocent as was his intent. "I have no idea what you are talking about. Who are you looking for? No one is here; no one has been here except a few patients yesterday. How did you even find me?"

"Sophia, my aunt. And she had a woman with her. Where are they?"

"Sophia! What makes you think she would be here? I haven't seen your aunt in quite a while. Is she ill? Does she need a doctor?"

"What were you doing at the Internet café in town this morning? I saw you on the news," Enrico said, ignoring the doctor's question.

"Oh, good heavens! Is that what this is all about? You saw me on the news! My computer went out on me. I went into town to input patient information on a flash drive while it was still fresh in my mind. See for yourself, it's all there in the folder," Andres said, pointing to the manila folder he'd dropped on the table when he entered the kitchen. While I was there, some thugs attacked a woman customer, and the police were called. That's the beginning and the end of it.

"Why am I telling you this if you saw it on the news? Once again, Enrico, what are you doing here? What do you want from me?"

Enrico's eyes narrowed. "Let me see your phone!"

Andres dug in his pocket for his cell phone. He watched as Enrico scrolled through his call log. Finally, he nodded and handed the phone back to the doctor. "I'm sorry for disrupting your day, Doctor."

Still in his role-model posture, Andres said, "Wait, wait, Enrico! At least tell me what's wrong. If I can help you, I will. Is Sophia ill? I don't understand any of this," he said fretfully.

"I'm trying to find my aunt." Enrico tapped his head to indicate his aunt had lost her marbles. "She's on the loose with some strange woman. If I find her, I will bring her to you to see if you can help her."

"You must be beside yourself. Sophia was more a mother to you than your own mother. She changed your diapers, fed you, helped you with your schoolwork, walked you to school, then met you to bring you home. She cooked for you and took care of you when you were sick.

"I can see how devastated you are. Take my telephone number, and if you need me, I will come to you. Will you do that?"

Enrico bit down on his bottom lip. Andres wasn't sure, but he thought he saw a tear form in the corner of his eye. In a voice that was rough and ragged, he said, "I'll do that, Doctor."

The moment the door closed behind Enrico, Andres sat down because his legs had finally given out. He dropped his head between his knees as he struggled to take deep breaths. Finally, when he was breathing normally, Andres shouted to the empty kitchen. "I pulled it off! I did it! Now, where the hell are you, Sophia?"

The doctor knew that someplace in his house was a clue. After all he'd gone through, Sophia wouldn't take Annie without leaving him a means to contact them. He went through his house as fast as he could, his gaze everywhere as he looked for a clue. When he saw the child's drawing in his surgery, his fist shot in the air. He stared at the stick child, the dog, and the cat in the drawing. Something was in the child's hand. What? What? His eyes dropped to the two animals. He burst out laughing when he saw the printed English words in a bubble over the dog's head. *What's news?* Not "new" but "news" with an *s*. He looked at the bubble over the cat's head. He frowned at the words he was seeing. He threw his hands in the air. *Home no news.* Home? No news at home? What did it mean?

The drawing in hand, Andres made his way back to the kitchen, where he sat down at the table to finish his coffee. It was cold. He hated cold coffee. He rinsed the pot and brewed a fresh pot. Then he would go back to town and call and e-mail all the people on Annie's list to inform them of this recent development. And tell them what? That Annie was gone, and he didn't know where she was?

Maybe Annie's friends would understand the stick drawing. He could scan it to them and see what they thought. Still, Sophia obviously thought he was smart enough to figure out the clue, so he should be able to figure it out.

Andres rubbed at his temples. Maybe by the time he drove back to the café, he would have it figured out. He clenched his jaw at the thought he could fail Sophia and Annie if he didn't come up with an answer.

Andres didn't realize how cold he was until the hot coffee streamed through his body. He poured a second cup and sipped it slowly as he let his thoughts go in all directions. Home? Home? Sophia's house. Did she go back there? He wasn't even sure where that home was, so he couldn't go there. Maybe it meant Annie's home. Well, he didn't know where that was, either. The mountain? Neither one of them could make it up that mountain. Home? The house where Enrico and his brothers grew up in? No, that had been sold long ago, and a new family lived there. Where was home? Whose home?

It hit him like a bolt of lightning. The one place Enrico wouldn't look for Sophia was his *own home*. Of course! How stupid he was. He should have thought of that first. He must truly be getting old.

How smart of Sophia to head there. The woman was a genius. He had a vague idea where Enrico lived. On a tree-lined boulevard. A high-rent district. He couldn't remember where or how he knew even that much.

Andres walked to his back door and looked out to check the weather. It was still raining but not as hard. He checked the time. If he left now to return to town, he would probably make good time. People would be returning to work after the lunch hour, which meant less traffic on the roads.

Andres walked to the hall closet and rummaged till he found a heavy, hooded jacket. He slipped it on and headed out the door for a return trip to town.

The traffic was light, just as he thought. He arrived in town in thirty minutes, but this time he had to park at the end of the street, which was a healthy walk to the Internet café. That was all right since he needed the exercise. He grinned as he found himself checking out the few pedestrians milling about with umbrellas. He didn't see anyone who looked like they didn't belong.

The bell over the door tinkled when Andres opened the door. Stephanie looked up and smiled. "You're back, Doctor!"

"Yes, I forgot something. Is there a computer available?"

"Not at the moment. But number seven will be free in fifteen minutes if you don't mind waiting."

"I don't mind at all. I thought your father was coming in after his dental appointment."

Stephanie laughed. "I thought so, too, but he was in such pain he went home. Mama said it was all right. I've been studying between dealing with the customers, and today, with the weather, business is pretty light."

"Tell me something, Stephanie, are you good with computers?"

"That depends on what you mean by good. I think so. What do you need help with?"

"I'm trying to locate someone. I know he lives in a high-rent area off a tree-lined boulevard. I'm not even sure how I know that. Do you know how I can locate him?"

Stephanie nodded as she started to tap away at the computer on the counter. "I need a name, Doctor."

Andres spelled out Enrico's first and last name. He waited, hardly daring to breathe. Could this young girl get him what he needed? Could it be that easy? He tapped his foot impatiently as Stephanie's fingers flew over the keys. He sighed as he eyed the clocks on the wall. Then his gaze swept over to the number seven station to see if the customer was finishing up. He sighed again when he saw how intent the young man was at what he was doing. With his luck, the man would sign on for more time.

Stephanie's fist shot in the air. I think I have it, Dr. Miguel! There is an Enrico Araceli on Avenue Belita. The number is 1102. His apartment number is 809. I think they are all condominiums on the boulevard. Very expensive to live there. My sister has a friend who lives there, so I guess that's where I heard that."

"Wonderful! Wonderful! Could you please write the address down for me? And one other thing, can I use your phone to make an international call?" Andres had his credit card in hand in a second.

And in that second, Dr. Andres Miguel almost had heart failure. He'd forgotten to bring the folder with him when he left the house. "The number, Doctor?"

The stricken look on Andres's face caused Stephanie to laugh out loud. "You forgot it, right?" Andres's head bobbed up and down. How could he have been so stupid? How?

"It's not a problem, Doctor. I can pull up the call log. No one has made any international calls since you made yours earlier today. You are like my father; he is not digitally inclined. Ah, here it is! Shall I call it for you?"

Andres grew so light-headed he had to grasp the end of the counter. The feeling passed as he reached for the phone. He walked over to the little desk in the corner. He sat down, the phone glued to his ear. His heart fluttered in his chest when the phone rang seven times without a connection. He was about to end the call when he heard the same voice he'd heard earlier. Andres jumped right in.

"This is Dr. Andres Miguel. The situation here has changed." He quickly rattled off his visit with Enrico, what had transpired, and informed the person on the other end of the line that he was back at the Internet café. "I think I know where Annie and Sophia went. I can't be certain, but it is the only thing that makes sense. I think Annie and Sophia are on their way to Enrico's condo. I have the address. It's 1102 Avenue Belita. His apartment number is 809. Tell me how long it will take you to get there?"

"This is Charles Martin, Doctor. I can't thank you enough for all your help. Right now we are about two hours, my people tell me, from your home."

"No, no. You must turn around and come this way. That to me means you are about three hours from where I am right now. From the café where I am, it is a forty-minute walk, possibly more, to Enrico's condominium. By now I'm thinking both women are there. I have no idea how they will have gained access, but your Annie is a very ingenious woman."

"Yes, she is. This might surprise you, but Annie is an expert at picking locks. She is also a crack shot with a gun. In other words, a woman of many talents. Is she okay?"

"For the most part, yes, Mr. Martin, Annie is okay. She is worried about her friend Myra. Is Myra all right?"

"Myra is with us. We're on our way, Doctor."

"I am going to try to find my way to Enrico's home. I don't know what good I will be, but I have to try. Don't tell me to stay put. I cannot do that. The number here at this Internet café should come up on your call record. If you need to reach me for whatever reason, call this number. The young lady can then get in touch with me on our local phone. Do you understand what I just said?"

"Yes, Doctor, I understand. Be careful. We're on our way. Be sure to tell Annie, if you get to her first, that *all* of us are here."

"I'll tell her," Andres said as he broke the connection. He walked back to Stephanie and handed her the phone. He explained what he needed her to do.

She wrote down his cell phone number carefully in an open ledger on the counter next to the computer. "Is there anything else I can help you with today? Number seven signed on for another hour; I'm sorry." She slid the charge slip across the counter for him to sign.

"Well, unless you have a gun there under the counter, I'm good." The startled look on the young girl's face stunned him. "Do you have one?" he hissed.

"I . . . I don't . . . but Papa has one. It's loaded, too," she whispered in return. "What is going on, Doctor? The police this morning and now . . . this!"

"Call your father and ask him if you can give me the gun. I'll be sure to return it to you. Please do this for me, Stephanie. It's important, but I can't . . . I can't tell you any more. Do it quickly, please."

Stephanie nodded and walked away, her fingers tapping the keys. Andres sucked in his breath and waited. He let it out and let loose with a sigh of relief when he saw her nod. She whirled around, placed the phone in its docking station, bent over, rummaged beneath the counter, and when she stood upright, she had a manila envelope in her hands. A *bulky* manila envelope in her hand. She slid it across the counter.

"One more thing, Stephanie, then I am out of your hair. Tell me the best route to Avenue Belita. I'll be walking. And be sure to thank your father for me."

"I'll write out the best route for you to take." Andres accepted the slip of paper, then walked behind the counter to hug the young girl, who was trembling so bad he hugged her tighter.

"Everything is fine. Nothing more is going to happen here. Thank you for all your help."

"You be careful, Doctor."

Andres nodded.

Outside the café, Andres realized that the temperature had dropped alarmingly. He pulled up the zipper on his jacket and tied the hood securely under his chin. It was still drizzling, but the worst of the rain was over. He walked steadily, his head down. He only raised his head when he reached a corner to look at a street sign before deciding if he was to go left or right. He plodded on.

It was dark now, the shops closing for the day, merchants lowering the steel grilles that covered the fronts of their shops. The sodium vapor lamps came on casting a bluish light over the boulevard. He looked up once he had passed the shops to a row of condominiums as he searched out 1102. He wanted to shout at the top of his lungs when he spotted the twelve-inch-high illuminated numbers.

Now, how was he to gain access to the lobby? He spotted a bell and pressed it. He could see into the well-lit, extravagantly appointed lobby. A young man looked up to see who was ringing the bell. Suddenly, Andres heard a voice coming from a tiny grille next to the bell. "Can I help you, sir?"

"Yes, my name is Dr. Andres Miguel. I'm

here to see my patient, Enrico Araceli. Please
let me in so I can see to him. He resides in
apartment 809."

The young man flipped open a book on his
desk, his finger moving down a list of names.
He nodded and pressed a button that opened
the door. Andres breathed a sigh of relief. He
had his medical identification in his hand that
the young man scrutinized carefully before he
handed it back. He then asked Andres to sign
a log-in sheet, which he did with misgivings.

"I didn't know Mr. Araceli was in residence.
I haven't seen him in over two weeks."

"Yes, he's back, and he's sick. He's been trying to doctor himself, and it didn't work, so
here I am."

"Where's your medical bag?" the young man
asked suspiciously, his eyes narrowing slightly.

Where, indeed. Andres panicked. "In my
car. I'm not staying. I'm taking Enrico to the
clinic. I parked outside the garage area. We'll
take the service elevator. If I need your help,
can I count on you? Mr. Araceli is a big man.
I'm an old man. So, young man, can I count
on you?"

The young man seriously pondered the question before he replied. "Yes, of course, Doctor.
Just call me. He scratched a phone number on a
sticky note and handed it over. The elevator is
to your right."

Andres scurried as fast as he could to the elevator, his heart pounding in his chest. He
clutched the manila envelope with the gun
close to his chest. He wondered how in the

world a gun could feel comforting. He had never in his life, not a single time, handled a gun.

Andres leaned against the elevator wall as he tried to get his breathing to level off. He bounded forward the moment the doors slid open. He looked up at the lighted arrows and numbers. He turned right; then he was standing in front of Enrico Araceli's door. He raised the door knocker and gave it three sharp knocks. He wasn't surprised when nothing happened. He put his mouth up against the door and shouted his name. He looked around to see if his outburst had roused anyone. Silence.

He waited a few minutes. Nothing.

Andres raised the knocker again and shouted his name at the same time. He literally fell inward when the door opened. Annie caught him as he was about to hit the floor.

"What took you so long?" Annie quipped.

"I have a gun!" Andres laughed, as he straightened up and handed over the manila envelope like it was the Holy Grail.

"Oh, you dear, sweet man, this is just what we need. I can't wait to shoot someone."

Andres believed her. "All your friends are here in Spain and on the way here to this very condo. I'm thinking three hours till they arrive. Your friend Myra is with them, and she's fine. I spoke to someone named Charles Martin."

"Ah. That's the best news I've heard in months."

"Now what do we do?" Sophia asked.

"Now we wait for the cavalry," Annie said.

Chapter 11

The meeting room, as it was called in the hotel, was small, with occupancy for only eight. With the gang all in attendance except for Avery Snowden's people, the group was as Dennis put it, squashed like sardines. "And," he went on to elaborate, "it's not called a hotel, it's called a *pensione*. It's a European term."

Alexis shot him a withering look and shook her head. She mouthed the words, *Tell that to someone who cares.* Dennis clamped his lips tight.

Charles blew his whistle, which he was never without, one sharp, earsplitting blast of sound. "We now have a new development," he said, pointing to the sat phone he was holding high in the air. "That call was from the good doctor named Andres Miguel. Annie and the woman named Sophia left the doctor's house. That means Annie and Sophia are on the run again.

The long and short of the story is that Enrico Araceli, who is obsessed with watching the news, spotted the doctor at the Internet café when the police were called to deal with a situation where a woman was accosted by some thugs. The doctor assumes that Enrico had stationed his thugs there to watch to see if Annie and Sophia would show up. He said the woman did resemble Annie. The young girl in charge dialed the emergency number, and the thugs were arrested. The doctor put two and two together and figured it all out when he returned home to find both women gone. Sophia, however, left a clue, and he's following up on it as I tell you this."

Everyone in the room started to jabber at once. "Where? Where does he think they went?" Myra's voice was the loudest, the shrillest.

"To Enrico Araceli's condominium. The doctor, who is not, by any means, a computer expert, had the young girl, who he said he delivered at birth, search the records, and she came up with Enrico's address. We now have the address. If any of you have questions about what I learned from the good doctor, I can't answer them. I just told you everything I know about what he told me. What we need to do now is make a plan and execute it."

"It's dark out now, and we're in a strange country. We don't know our way around here," Isabelle said.

"We've operated under worse conditions," Nikki shot back. "I am totally against waiting for morning in case that is your idea of a plan."

Cyrus, who was under the table because there was no room for him topside, barked a short blast of sound. His whole body was quivering from head to toe. He wanted *out* of here, and he wanted out *now!*

"I hear you, buddy," Jack said as he opened the door of the meeting room and stepped outside, Cyrus on his heels. The others followed down a short hallway, which led to an outdoor exit, where they all gathered under a portico of sorts. It gave them a little elbow room, but not by much.

"My people are on the way to the Village of Tears," Charles said. "Our MO is we're a hiking club. It's the same story we gave the desk clerk here at the hotel. If the village is under siege, my people will know it in an instant. They are in a rental van, and just to make sure our story holds, I had them rent enough mountain-climbing gear for all of us. That was the plan before this last call, when we all thought Annie would possibly head there. I have no other information other than Enrico's profile, which we got from his place of business, a few friends, and one old neighbor whose memory was faulty at best. Just for the record, the only way to climb the mountain is from the base. It's a one-road-in and one-road-out location."

"Tell us again what you found out," Maggie said.

"Enrico Araceli, which means 'altar of heaven,' is pretty much a loner. Sees himself as head of his family, which consists of two brothers who were born ten months apart and consider themselves twins, and Sophia, who is his mother's sister. He did exceptionally well in school, his brothers, not so much. He was obsessed with money from an early age, and it was only natural for him to make his living in the financial world. Thanks, our sources said, to his uncle Armand. I alerted Abner back home, and he was able to hack into Enrico's personal banking records. His net worth is around two million dollars U.S., in different bank accounts.

"His portfolio is quite impressive. He has another two or three million in stocks and bonds. He owns the condo, which is high-end and worth close to a million dollars. He drives a Ferrari. Buys only designer clothing. There are no known serious female relationships in his life. Dinner dates, mostly business. As one of his colleagues put it, Enrico is not the sharing type, and if he had a wife, a mistress, he'd have to share. A female colleague told one of my operatives she made *a move* on him only to find out he had severe hang-ups on the mother issue, and she bolted. She didn't want any part of *that*.

"Enrico attended the university and is supposedly quite smart. The brothers did not attend the university. Both of them are what passes for normal. They're mechanics. They have good jobs and make a decent wage. They bank most of their money except for living expenses. They share a garden apartment. They know how to cook and take care of themselves. One of them is in a relationship that will lead to marriage down the road. They're as close as twins can be even though they aren't twins. Supposedly there is no love or admiration for their brother Enrico. They do, however, recognize that he is the head of the family, and as is the custom here, they obey the head of the family, whether they like it or not.

"I wasn't able to get much on Count de Silva, Annie's husband. No one mentioned that he was impoverished; they were all in awe of the title. Until his death, all three boys thought of him as Uncle Armand. He came and went like a visiting uncle. No one thought anything of it. And there was not one single person who would comment on the mother's three pregnancies. Maybe they thought they were miracle births, I simply do not know since there was no husband anywhere in the picture. At least not one that anyone could remember.

"We spoke to a few of Flavio's and Mateo's friends, who were very reticent to speak about the young men, even with cash being offered for information. We came away with the idea they are just two normal guys with no agendas other than getting from one day to the next.

"If they're in on this . . . whatever this is in regard to Annie, they were coerced. Oh, one other thing, both Flavio and Mateo are active in their church and, unlike Enrico, who only attends midnight mass on Christmas Eve, are good Catholics.

"His secretary told that to my operative. With a hundred euros in her hand, she also said he was a devil to work for and was obsessed with making money. She did say that he paid her well. She has two young girls she is supporting, and that's the only reason she puts up with his abuse."

"What's the situation with Annie's business manager? She ordered him to pay up so Enrico wouldn't harm the villagers. Is that still on the table now that Annie managed to get away?" Nikki asked.

"I haven't heard from Connor since the original call. I simply do not know. I don't even know if he knows that Annie broke free. I've called him twice, and both times the calls went to voice mail. I've left detailed messages. I'm still waiting to hear back from him. For all I know, he could be communicating directly with Enrico," Charles said. His frustration was evident in that he kept rubbing the stubble on his cheeks and chin.

"I'm freezing out here," Maggie grumbled. "It's raw and cold, and the drizzle is not going to go away anytime soon. We need to get this show on the road, guys."

The Sisters concurred by rubbing their hands together and stomping their feet. The boys started to move off in the direction of Avery Snowden's van, which sat in the middle of the parking lot like a lone lost soldier. The single lamp, high on a pole, cast a scary blue glow over the white van. The pavement was wet and slick with oil, and it glistened in the eerie blue light.

"It's settled, then," Myra said in a voice that held no room for argument. "The boys are going to the Village of Tears, and the rest of us are going into town to Enrico's apartment to rescue Annie. It's late now, so there shouldn't be that much traffic. We'll use the van Ted rented for us. The problem is what to do with all these mopeds."

"I'm on that," Dennis said. "I just e-mailed the rental company, and, for a fee, they will come and pick them up in the morning. We're good to go."

Cyrus barked his happiness as he sprinted to the white van. He was the first one aboard. He continued to bark his happiness until Harry told him to cool his jets, at which point Cyrus leaped up and wrapped his paws around the martial artist's neck and proceeded to lick his cheeks. In spite of himself, Harry laughed out loud. The tension eased among the group in an instant.

The women moved off toward the van, their heads down as they tried to avoid the stinging, wet, cold drizzle. When they reached the van, Kathryn, who was in the lead, opened the door. She looked around to see Charles and Fergus. "No, no! You two go with the boys. This is *our* mission. We can handle this."

Fergus squared his shoulders as he prepared to board the van as Charles sucked in his breath.

All it took was one hard, steely look from Myra and Yoko springing forward on her toes in the eerie light to make both men turn around and head to Avery Snowden's van.

"Women power! I like that." Isabelle giggled.

Kathryn settled herself behind the wheel. "Maggie, you ride shotgun. Program the GPS and we're good to go."

The Sisters settled in, buckled up, and whispered among themselves so as not to distract Kathryn, who drove the van like she drove her eighteen-wheeler.

Two hours later, Kathryn called out, "We're making good time, people. Another thirty minutes, and we'll make our destination. Decide how we're going to penetrate the building. Do we go in the front door, or do we go in through the garage?"

"I vote for the garage," Nikki called out loud enough for Kathryn to hear.

The Sisters concurred with Nikki, shouting out that they didn't need to look for trouble, and trouble was the front door, with its possible security guard.

"*We're coming, Annie. We're almost there,*" Myra muttered over and over to herself. She could hardly wait to wrap her arms around her old friend.

Forty minutes later, Kathryn slowed the van. "We're here, girls!" Maggie bellowed from the passenger seat.

The Sisters sat upright and unbuckled their seat belts on cue. They settled their backpacks firmly over their shoulders as they prepared to spring forward.

"This is not good," Kathryn shouted. "There's a grille that goes from top to bottom. I guess the residents have a keycard to raise the grille. What should we do?"

The Sisters conferred. There was no apparent solution.

"Back up and wait for someone to open it up. Be ready to follow right behind them. It's either that, or you crash through the gate, which will certainly bring the police," Nikki said.

Kathryn did as instructed, grumbling as she did so.

"Relax, I think people will be returning from their nights out soon. Just keep the engine running so you can follow right behind them," Myra said.

Exactly nineteen minutes later, a minivan slid to a stop. The security grille started to rise slowly. The low-slung minivan moved, Kathryn almost on the minivan's bumper.

"You did it! Good going, Kathryn," Yoko said as she raced to the front of the van. "Park in the first slot you see. We'll walk the rest of the way till we find an elevator."

"We're coming, Annie. We're almost there!" Myra whispered to herself.

Myra was second off the van as her gaze swept the garage for some sign of where the elevator might be. When she spotted the sign, she broke into a run, the Sisters behind her. She was breathless when she pressed the big red button to open the elevator door.

It wasn't a big elevator, but somehow they all managed to squeeze into the mahogany-walled square that would take them to where Annie waited.

"Fancy elevator. Even has a carpet," Isabelle said.

"And this is important, why?" Maggie shot back.

"It's not. I was just making conversation because I'm nervous. Is that okay with you, Miss Smartass Reporter?"

"Yeah, yeah. Sorry, Isabelle."

"No problem. Did anyone press the button?" No one had. Nikki pressed the button, and the elevator started to rise. The doors opened in a matter of seconds.

"Eighth floor! Annie is in 809. Let's go, girls!"

Myra led the rush. She was breathless when she reached the end of the hall, with 809 the last apartment on the right-hand side of the long hallway. She closed her fist and thumped the door, three sharp thumps. She looked up to see an eyeball staring at her. "Annie!"

The door started to open slowly, too slowly for Myra. She pushed it inward and screamed Annie's name.

"I can hear you, Myra!" Annie laughed as she hobbled to Myra and wrapped her arms around her best friend in the whole world. And then she held her arms open to welcome the others. Tears flowed as the women clung to each other.

"It must be a nice feeling to be loved like that," Sophia whispered to Dr. Miguel.

"I would think it's a wonderful feeling. I never felt love like that. I guess you haven't, either. It's a beautiful thing to see. We need to rejoice with them."

"Girls, girls, I want you to meet two wonderful people. I wouldn't be here if it weren't for them. Sophia, Andres, these are my friends from America, who came to rescue me. Myra, Nikki, Isabelle, Alexis, Maggie, Kathryn, and Yoko, meet Sophia and Dr. Andres Miguel."

Smiles, laughter, and handshakes followed. More chatter, a discussion about Annie's leg and the strange clothes she was wearing, which she explained belonged to Enrico Araceli. "I needed to take a shower, and I wanted clean clothes. Everything is cashmere, even these sweatpants. I didn't know there was such a thing as cashmere sweatpants. That skunk has expensive taste. These duds are brand-new, the tags were still on them; otherwise, I wouldn't be wearing them." Everyone laughed.

"What are you going to do now?" Sophia asked. "I don't know how safe we are here. I would suggest you go with your people, and Dr. Miguel and I will find someplace to go for the time being."

"Sophia is right," Myra said. "Annie, are you good to go?"

"I am. I won't hold you up."

"You need to give your leg a rest. Prop it up from time to time. Go now! I can't guarantee how long the curious reception clerk will remain quiet. For some reason I see him coming up here to see if Enrico is indeed here," Andres said.

Myra nodded. Annie was first at the door, then turned to hobble back. She hugged Sophia and Andres, hard. "'Thank you' hardly seems enough."

"It is enough. Go! Andres and I will be fine," Sophia said, her eyes flooding with tears.

More hugs, more handshakes, more tears, and the Sisters were gone as they scurried from the apartment, down the hall, and then down the stairs to the garage level.

"Where's Fergus?" Annie asked as she settled herself into her seat.

Nikki explained that the boys had gone ahead to the Village of Tears, along with Avery.

"Enrico is deranged. Did Connor pay my ransom?" Annie asked.

"We don't know," Myra said. "Charles said his calls went straight to voice mail."

Annie frowned as she tried to digest the information she was hearing. "Enrico took all my credentials and my sat phone, as well as Myra's. Can I borrow someone's phone? I need to make a few calls." Nikki handed over her special phone. The Sisters turned around to give Annie the privacy she needed to make her calls.

"Where are we going, girls?" Kathryn asked as she cranked the engine.

"The Village of Tears. Where else?" Nikki said.

"Maggie, do your thing with the GPS. We have a long drive ahead of us, people."

"There's one good thing about all of this. We're all together," Myra said happily as she stared at the back of Annie's head. "Right now, that's all that matters."

"Hear! Hear!" Alexis shouted.

Chapter 12

Avery Snowden cut the engine of his motorcycle, dismounted, and walked it the rest of the way into a grove of fig trees that was darker than midnight. He shook the rain from his windbreaker and rolled his shoulders to ease the tension from his long, wet ride here to the Village of Tears. "Talk to me," he barked to his six-person team, which consisted of four men and two women, as he entered the van that was sitting like a lone sentinel in the grove.

"The villagers are split up into three groups: at the church, the school, and the padre's residence. There are three men guarding the school. The two brothers are at the school, along with one other man. Enrico is at the rectory, with two thugs who he sends out from time to time. Right now he's alone inside with the priests. The people in the church are guarded by a six-man team.

"Other clusters of people, and that includes children, are being held in individual houses. We can't confirm the numbers. The town is dark. We were crawling around on our bellies, and there are dogs who bark incessantly. Not an ideal situation. The good news is that the rain muffled any sounds we made.

"The guards, for want of a better term, are what the locals would call wharf rats, thugs who will do anything for a few euros. They all have guns. A motley crew, to be sure. The dregs of humanity. Here you can buy guns very easily on the black market."

"Cell phone reception here is bad unless you have a sat phone like ours. This guy Enrico has one that appears to look like one of ours. It's possible it's Annie's or Myra's. It was hard to see in the dark even with the infrared lens. I would assume he's using either the one belonging to the countess or Mrs. Rutledge. You did say he confiscated theirs on their arrival. We had him in our sights when he stepped out to make a call, but it was impossible to hear his end of the conversation with the rain."

"How long ago did Melrose and Manza head out there?" Snowden asked.

"Forty minutes ago. They're using the night-vision gear. No one is out and about because of the weather. Sometimes, the wharf rats step out to smoke. We know which houses some of the people are in because the lights are on. The rest of the village is dark."

"Who else besides the two padres are in the rectory with Enrico?" Snowden asked.

"There's a middle-aged man, late forties. The two guards left a short while ago. I used our voice activator, but even so it was hard to hear. I think he's the mayor, the constable, the judge, and he's a lawyer. He wears all those hats, so he's more or less the head of the village. There's another young guy, a deputy of sorts, I think. I can't say if they had weapons or not. Even if they did, they would have been confiscated.

"It was very tense in there, I can tell you that. I was going to go back when you arrived. What do you want me to do? The old padre is not holding up too well, and the younger padre took a few cuffs to the head from Enrico. The big guy tried to intervene but got punched down by Enrico's threatening to shoot the old padre. He's deranged, boss."

"So you're saying there are three guns in the rectory."

"Yeah, boss, and that guy Enrico appears to want to shoot someone. He will, too. I don't see him being long on patience."

Snowden nodded. "Go! Be careful, Barker."

"Always, boss, always."

Snowden dropped his head into his hands. He dreaded Charles Martin's arrival, because he had very little to report. Sir Charles did not suffer fools. More to the point, he himself did not suffer fools, either, and that's exactly how he felt at the moment.

Snowden felt his phone vibrate in his

pocket. He pulled it out to see who the caller was. Charles. He took a long, deep breath and clicked it on. "Where are you?"

"Ninety minutes out if our calculations are right. Update, please."

Snowden made no excuses. He reported the facts as they had been reported to him. "We're hunkered in for the most part. The weather is foul, as you know. The only plus is we know where everyone is, at least for now. It appears that Enrico is losing patience. Unfortunately, we don't have ears on anything. Opticals aren't all that good, either. Dogs are barking incessantly. Any word on Annie and the others? Is she secure?"

"Annie is fine. The girls are on their way here. They're an hour behind us. Sit tight. Wait, one last question. Do you know how Enrico is communicating with his men? Are they using phones, or is he going from building to building?"

"They have phones. But Enrico did go to the school, where the two brothers are, along with one other guard. No real head count, but the school appears to be full."

The old spies signed off.

Snowden rolled his shoulders to ease the tension he was feeling. He needed to do something, and he needed to do it *now*. No way was he going to sit inside this van twiddling his thumbs for the next ninety minutes. He pawed through his rucksack, searching for the special dog spray he and all his operatives carried. It was a special concoction that would fell an animal for forty-five minutes but would not harm the animal in a permanent way. Even though there were no reports of dogs roaming around or even tied up outside, he couldn't afford to take any chances. He jammed the canister into one of the pockets of his cargo pants. He continued to transfer different articles to the other pockets. He didn't want to be encumbered if he had to drop to his belly and crawl around in the muck.

"Stay sharp," he ordered to his two remaining operatives as he exited the van. He looked around to get his bearings. He was glad it was dark, but he hated the bone-chilling wetness that slapped at him square in the face. He shrugged it off as he moved forward, careful to stay in the clusters of trees that dripped heavy rain.

Avery approached the entrance to the village. He had on his night-vision goggles. The simple sign declaring the village's name appeared to have been carved by a master craftsman and had weathered well over time. Everything in his line of vision was green.

The village was totally dark except for five or six pinpoints of yellow light spilling out of the windows in the buildings where the villagers were being held.

He knew that in the bright light of day, with the sun shining, this little village was the same as many small towns in Middle America. He knew the villagers took care of their little houses, maintained their gardens and yards. He clearly remembered Annie once describing the village and what she had done to bring it into the modern world. Somewhere, there was a town square for local festivities. He clearly remembered her saying the church glistened in the bright sun. She'd also said the church was peaceful, the pews polished to a high sheen. She'd said it smelled like candle wax and found it comforting. She'd prayed there often after the death of her family at sea.

Snowden moved stealthily as he chose the school as his target. He wasn't sure, but he thought the two brothers might be the weak link in their brother's operation. He hoped he wasn't wrong. A minute later, he made the decision that eyes on was his choice of action. Sometimes body language was almost better than a verbal conversation.

Avery stopped dead in his tracks when he felt something brush up against his leg. He looked down through his night-vision goggles that had turned the world green to see a soaking-wet cat trying to crawl up his leg. Some child's pet. He didn't stop to think; he bent down, scooped it up, then slid the drenched cat inside his windbreaker. The cat, a little bigger than a kitten, squirmed, jiggled, then found a comfortable spot and glued itself to Avery's flannel shirt. It meowed softly. Avery found himself smiling as he moved forward, surprised at how comforting the cat felt nestled against his chest.

Snowden moved slowly, his gaze sweeping the driveway and the narrow paths that led up to the schoolroom doors. Back in the States, this little schoolhouse would be considered a country school, with small rooms and small classes and teachers who weren't certified. Although Annie said several of the young people she had sent to the university had returned to the village to teach. He hoped that was the case since education was so vital in this day and age.

Four steps led to the thick, wide, plank door, with hinges that looked like they belonged to some medieval structure back in the days of moats and castles. Snowden assumed that the same sorts of hinges would be on the inside to secure the doors and were inevitably in place.

He stayed in the trees as he made his way back along the side to what he assumed was a back door and playground. He allowed himself a smile as he felt the little cat snuggle more deeply against him. He or she must be feeling his body warmth. The thought pleased him enormously. He hoped some child wasn't crying for the loss of his or her pet. He made a silent promise to himself not to leave the area until he reunited the cat with its person.

Snowden stood silently, staring at the back entrance of the school. The back door was a replica of the front door, thick planks with monster hinges. The word *fortress* came to mind. He stared now at the row of windows, with their sickly yellow light, green to him now. It took a moment for him to realize there was some kind of glaze on the windows, which meant that even if he were standing directly in front of it, he wouldn't be able to see a thing. What to do?

Instinct kicked in when the back door groaned open and two men stepped out under the small overhang. Cigarette time. Snowden stepped deeper into the copse of trees. He fumbled for his high-tech listening device and held it in front of him, but not before he inserted two tiny buds in his ears. The cat inside his wind-breaker squirmed. His hand massaged the wiggling animal, and it calmed immediately.

The conversation was in Spanish. He struggled to hear and understand what they were saying. He squinted to make sure it was the two brothers and not the wharf rats. Satisfied, he concentrated on what was being said.

"I hate this place. I hate what Rico is doing. We should leave, Mateo. He can't force us to stay here. I don't like holding a gun. I hate guns. Why are we still here?"

"We're here because we're both stupid. He says do this, do that, and we do it. We're his puppets. That was fine when we were kids, but not now. I can't believe he's doing this. These people have done nothing to him, and he's threatening to kill them. He's sick in his head," Flavio grumbled.

"I can tell you one thing—I am not shooting anyone. I took the bullets out of the gun. That dimwit inside will shoot anyone who looks at him the wrong way. I think we should take him out. He's looking tired to me. His reflexes are off. We can tie him up and shove him into that broom closet. If Rico comes looking for him, all we say is that he left to smoke or to take a leak and didn't come back. I'm game if you are," Mateo said.

"He'll just send another of the rats from the church. I think there are twelve in total."

Flavio digested his brother's words. "Then we'll take him out, too," Mateo said.

Snowden watched as both brothers smoked in silence for a minute or two.

"I think I could shoot Rico. I really do, Mateo. I am so sick and tired of him and his obsessions. He really is sick in his head. The countess seemed like a nice lady, a kind lady. She's a victim here, just like all these village people. I will not have any part of hurting those two priests. I will not. Do you hear me, Mateo?"

"Of course I can hear you. Rico has no soul. If we shoot him, we'll be in confession every day for the rest of our lives. He has the Devil's blood running in his veins.

"If we turn him over to the authorities, all he has to do is flash those special badges he showed us. He said those things were a 'get out of jail free' card, whatever that means. There is no doubt in my mind that he'll blame the two of us for everything. I don't want to go to jail, and neither do you. I'm prepared to walk away from here right now, right this minute if you're game."

Mateo tossed his cigarette into a puddle. He watched it sizzle, then fizzle out.

"No, we have to take a stand and let this play out the way it's meant to play out. Rico wants to be legitimate. He can't come to terms with the fact that it is impossible. There is no longer royalty. No one cares in this day and age. He can't accept that our mother was a lady of the evening, either. How did the two of us get to be so smart, Flavio?"

Flavio made a strangled sound deep in his throat. "You know the answer to that, brother. We have a different father. We don't have his father's ugly blood running through our veins. How many times did Rico beat our asses when we were kids when we brought that up? He's all mixed up in his head. He still believes our mother was some kind of princess queen, and the count was his father, and the two of us are just guttersnipes. He will never ever believe anything different."

"Too many to count. I still have the scars." Flavio's cigarette followed his brothers. "We need to go back inside."

Snowden's eyes almost popped out of his head behind the night-vision goggles. Had he just heard what he heard? As Jack Emery was fond of saying, he didn't see that coming. Well, damn. How could he have missed what he'd just heard? Or was it a family secret that only the Aracelis knew about? He could hardly wait to get back to the van to call Charles. The little cat moved, snuggled closer to his armpit, and then meowed softly.

The brothers weren't the count's spawn. There was no love lost between the three brothers. In fact, the two of them thought their brother was deranged. Allies. But how to bring that about. Once a new day arrived and the bright light of day surfaced, moving around would be impossible. Well, there were still many hours of darkness ahead. Hours to plan and plot and *act*.

The little cat inside his windbreaker continued to meow in contentment.

As Snowden made his way back to the van, his thoughts turned Stateside and what Abner Tookus was doing. And Annie's business manager.

Back in the States, Abner Tookus turned his special phone to speaker mode and propped it up on his desk so he could continue tapping away at his computer. "I'm on it, Connor," he muttered to Annie's business manager. "I understand everything you said in your last four frantic phone calls. You need to remember who you are talking to here. Plus, I told you that I enlisted the aid of the world's number one hacker, Philonias Needlemeyer. I admit I don't know what all you had to do to liquidate Annie's holdings. Having said that, I appreciate all you did and are still doing. I got it! We are good to go. The minute you alert me that you are about to transfer that humungous amount of money into Enrico Araceli's brokerage account, my finger will be on the key to transfer it out. Both transactions will take less than a minute. Araceli will see it; then it will be gone. He will think it's a glitch. We will then send it back, let it lie for a moment, and when he sees that it stays put, that's when we make our final move. I got it, Connor."

Abner listened as the business manager droned on. "You do have that right; Annie will kill you if you screw this up. It will be me next on her list. I have no desire to end up dead, so you can rest easy. We're good here, Connor?" Abner laughed at Connor's shaky response.

Abner leaned back in his ergonomic chair and held his index finger high in the air. He wiggled it every which way to make sure it was limber enough to press the key that would transfer half of Annie's vast fortune to her dead husband's illegitimate son. Now that was a mind-blower to be sure.

Abner bolted forward when he saw he had a call coming in from his wife, Isabelle.

Their greeting over, he asked where she was.

"We rescued Annie and now we're on our way to meet up with the boys and Mr. Snowden. The meeting place is the middle of a fig grove. Enrico is holding the whole village hostage and is threatening to kill the two priests. His two brothers are there, too. We still don't know how we're going to rescue everyone. We're all counting on you, honey, to make this work."

Abner wiggled his finger and nodded, forgetting that his wife couldn't see him. "I'm good to go, just waiting for Connor's call. Tell that to Annie. I won't let you down."

The conversation turned to, do you miss me, I miss you, yada yada.

"Gotta go. Myra is giving me the evil eye. Love you."

"And I love you," Abner whispered, until he realized he was talking to dead air.

"Okay, you son of a bitch, let's see how smart you are," Abner mumbled under his breath as he tapped into Enrico Araceli's brokerage account again. He pondered the amount as he calculated how to reduce the bottom line to zero one more time.

Abner laughed out loud. A piece of cake.

Chapter 13

Snowden was halfway back to the van when he changed his mind, whirled around, and headed toward the rectory, the cat nestled next to his chest meowing softly at his abrupt movement. It was raining harder now, drenching him but muffling all sound. He hated that his feet were soaking wet and cold as he sloshed his way toward the rectory. Instinct told him something was happening inside the small cottage that consisted of four rooms and one and a half baths, the place where the two priests lived. He couldn't remember who had told him about the cottage's layout. Obviously, the information came from someone his operatives had spoken to along the way when they practiced their due diligence.

Two bedrooms, obviously, since two priests lived in the house. Probably a sitting room that doubled as an office, and a kitchen. There would be no need for a parlor or general room since priests, as a rule, didn't entertain.

A front door. A back door. The back door was probably off the kitchen, possibly some space for a laundry. Even priests had to do laundry. Maybe he could pick the lock and sneak in. And do what?

Snowden groaned out loud, causing the little cat to meow louder when he slipped in a dip in the ground. He was up to his knees in muck. Then he cursed. The cat moved and tried its best to snuggle into his armpit. *Stupid, Avery,* he chastised himself. He looked around to get his bearings. He shook his head to clear the rain from his face. He slipped his night-vision goggles on again and slogged forward, confident that even if he was making noise, it couldn't be heard indoors over the sound of the pelting rain.

Snowden inched his way toward the back door and the single diamond-paned window. He was reminded of the Hansel and Gretel cottage from childhood fairy tales. He was glad that, unlike the schoolhouse, this building's windows were clear glass and not glazed. He was adjusting his goggles when he froze in place. He wasn't sure, but he thought he felt a warm breath on his neck.

"Boss, what are you doing here?"

"Making the rounds," Snowden hissed in return. He must be slipping. He should have picked up on Barker's heat signature. "You got anything?"

"Two guys tied to chairs. The two priests are mobile. The older one is pretty much just sitting. The younger one is pacing and praying his rosary. Araceli keeps his phone busy. He's made a lot of calls. He seems to be checking something, like every few minutes. No way to tell exactly, and I sure as hell can't read lips. Things look tense. Oh, and just for the record, that's an automatic weapon he's got. No sign of any guards."

"So what you're saying is he could mow down everyone in the room before we could break down either the front or back door."

"That's what I'm saying, boss. What do you want to do here?"

"Nothing right now. We have to wait for the boys to get here. Then we'll make our decisions. At least we know Araceli hasn't carried through on his threat to shoot anyone." Snowden went on to tell his operative what he'd overheard at the schoolhouse.

Barker shook his head, then swiped his face with the back of his hand. "That's the best news I've heard since we got here. There's nothing going on here, and I doubt anything will go on before morning. We stay out here, we're both going to come down with pneumonia. I'm just saying, boss."

Snowden nodded. "Let's go back to the van and get into some dry clothes. The rain is getting colder, so I see your point. There's nothing worse than getting sick in a foreign country." To back up his words, he whirled around and started to slog his way around the rectory and out to the road that would take them back to the heated van.

Barker quickly turned on the heater as both men started to strip down. Both rummaged for clean, dry clothes in the mountain of gear loaded in the back of the van.

Barker's eyes almost popped out of his head when he heard the little cat protest at being removed from its warm nest next to the boss's chest. His jaw dropped when he saw his boss cuddle the animal, but not before he cooed in its ear. Wait till he shared this with the guys and gals in Snowden's employ. Even the boss was human after all. The thought pleased him.

Dressed in thermal underwear with heavy-duty cords and a thick flannel shirt, Snowden looked down at the little cat, then scooped it up and returned it to its temporary home against his chest. Later, he would think about the peaceful feeling he felt when the cat purred its thanks. He wondered if it was a girl or a boy cat, not that it made a difference. He looked over at Barker, daring him to make a comment, which the operative knew better than to do.

"What now, boss?"

"Like you said, nothing is going to go on now, so we just wait. At least we're warm and dry for the moment," Snowden said, as he held out a large plastic bag for Barker to dump his wet clothes in, along with his boots. He cinched the bag and tossed it in the back. "Catch a few winks if you can."

The old spy settled himself in one of the

van's seats and stretched out. The little cat was still purring in contentment. His thoughts turned to the mission he was on as he recalled every move he and his people had made since their arrival in Spain. So far, they hadn't made any mistakes. Not knowing the two brothers' true heritage didn't come under the heading of a mistake, but he could see how it was going to play a big part in the resolution of this particular mission.

Snowden closed his eyes, knowing he wouldn't doze or fall asleep. He always did his best thinking with his eyes closed for some reason. He opened his eyes and looked down at the watch on his wrist, which did everything but cook a meal. Charles and his gang should be arriving anytime now. He closed his eyes again.

Twenty minutes later, Barker stirred and called out, "Company, boss."

Within minutes, the oversize van was full and steamed up, with everyone jabbering at once. Charles yanked at his whistle and gave it a sharp blast. The little cat stirred, squirmed, and snuggled deeper against Snowden's chest. Obviously, it knew friends from foes. That was a good thing, Snowden decided.

"This is the situation, boys. Annie's business manager, Connor, has been in constant contact with me and has a virtual open line to Enrico Araceli, who is rapidly losing patience with him. He keeps threatening to shoot the two priests. He even went so far as to say the old priest had outlived his usefulness, so it would be no great loss. He's now given Connor a deadline to transfer what he considers his share of Annie's holdings to his own account in Barcelona. Abner is on it and knows exactly what to do.

"But that's not the end of it. He's demanding Annie show herself at the rectory so she can draft a letter that he's going to send around the world. Those are his words, *around the world,* so the entire world will know he is the son of Count Armand de Silva. Obviously, he does not understand or refuses to understand that people could care less. The man is deranged, plain and simple."

"What is Annie saying?" Snowden asked.

"They're an hour out the last I heard from them. Annie is willing to do whatever it takes to make sure the villagers are safe. The letter is a joke, but not to Enrico. He's obsessed with the world's knowing who he is. The bottom line, of course, is that the world doesn't care, and he can't see that after such a letter is released, he will be a laughingstock. That's how obsessed he is with his lineage.

"And I also think from all we now know, there's a problem with his mother. He refuses to acknowledge . . . how do I say this . . . her free-spirited ways. He knows what she was, but if he doesn't speak of it, then it doesn't matter. And now you tell us what you overheard the other two brothers say. Which just confirms the nature of the mother's . . . ah . . . professional life," Charles said.

"The bottom line is that Annie will head for the rectory the moment they get here. So we need to come up with a plan as to what we're going to do before that happens. We do not want any bloodshed if we can help it. We all need to be aware of Araceli's mental state at all times."

Jack spoke up. "There's no room in this van for all of us. Charles and Fergus can stay here, and the rest of us will go back to our van to wait for the girls. Unless you think there's something we can do."

"Sounds good. We'll call the minute we know something," Snowden said.

"Is our plan for Harry and me to show up at the door at first light as two mountain climbers still on the table, or did you switch it up?" Jack asked.

Snowden nodded. "It's still on the table unless things change when the girls get here. You might as well take the climbing gear with you now."

Mass confusion ensued as everyone jostled everyone else in their haste to get outside, so the gear Jack and Harry would need could be found.

"This sucks," Dennis mumbled as he ran for the van they'd arrived in.

"You got that right, kid," Ted said, pummeling him on the back.

"How am I supposed to take pictures in this slop?" Espinosa groused.

Jack laughed out loud. "We'll all pose for you when we get back to the van. My publicity kit could use a few new pictures. My right side is my good side, so make sure you capture it accurately, and be sure the lighting is on my side."

"Eat shit, Jack," Espinosa barked as he slammed open the door of the van. He shook himself like a shaggy, wet dog, rainwater going in all directions.

"Already I hate that guy Araceli, and I haven't even met him yet?" Ted snarled. "He's sitting in that rectory like the king of the hill, and the rest of us are here and miserable. I wonder what that sick bastard is doing right this minute."

What the sick bastard was doing at that moment was jamming the gun in his hand under Padre Santos Mendoza's chin. The old priest just stared at him with unblinking intensity. Even with the cataracts on his eyes, he could see the crazed stare of Enrico Araceli. He said nothing even though his heart was thumping wildly in his chest.

"I *will* kill you, you do know that, right?"

"If it is meant to be, then so be it. My death will be on your soul, and there will be no entrance to heaven for you. I am at peace with my Maker."

"Then maybe I should shoot this young one, who is so frantically praying on his beads. Or your constable, or his deputy. I don't think they're ready to meet their Maker quite yet," Araceli snarled

The old priest winced. He wanted to do

something, anything, to change what was going on, but he knew there was nothing he could do. Even if a weapon were to suddenly appear in his hands, he knew he could not use it. He prayed silently.

Tired of baiting the old priest, Enrico wandered to the far end of the kitchen, so he could study his phone in the dim light. He pressed the button on his speed dial that would connect him with Annie's business manager. There were no amenities. "Well?"

Connor's reply was curt. "As I told you a dozen times already, this cannot be done in your time frame. Suffice it to say it is being done, but it will be another few hours at least, with certainty by dawn your time. Now, stop calling me and taking up my time." Enrico blinked at the sudden ending of the call. He frowned. This was the first time since he'd connected one-on-one with the financial wizard that the man had talked back to him. Something was afoot. His eyes narrowed to mean slits. He could almost smell it. But what was it?

Enrico leaned against the wall, his gaze never leaving the two old priests except to glance down at the latest news reports, which he was obsessed with receiving. He got text alerts every few minutes. It was, to him, the fastest and only way to keep up with what he called life.

Nothing alarming. He walked over to the constable and his deputy. He stared at them for a full minute before he turned and walked back to the living area. The young priest was still fingering his beads. The old priest was dozing in his chair.

Things were too quiet. He called his men, his own private little army, to check in with how everything was progressing. Like he really cared if people were hungry or children were crying or people needed to use the bathroom. His last call was to his two derelict brothers. "Talk to me."

"You're an ass wipe, Rico," Mateo said.

"I'm going to have to teach you some respect very soon, Mateo. What's going on?"

"Your guard went out and never came back. But I guess you already know that, and that's why you're calling. How's that for talking?"

"What are you talking about? When did he leave?"

"Maybe half an hour ago. The man is an ass wipe like you are, so we really didn't do much talking. He didn't ask permission to go out; he just walked out the door, and he has not come back. I just checked to see if he was under the overhang smoking, but he isn't there. And don't even think about telling me to go out and look for him. If you are so concerned about him, do it yourself."

Enrico ended the call and immediately called the guard in question. The call went straight to voice mail. Crap. He didn't even know the man's name. He was just one of the crew he'd signed on for 300 euros. He left a curt message, then tried the number again, with the same results. Something was up. He'd sensed it earlier. Mutiny?

Doubtful, since no one had been paid as yet. The thought that his two brothers might somehow be involved floated through his head. No, they were cowards. They'd never cross or betray him, they were family.

Then what?

Chapter 14

The van was crowded and steamy, with the heater running at full blast. The temperature gauge said the outdoor temperature was thirty-seven degrees. Tempers were short, with Cyrus's the shortest. He wanted action, not lying under a seat that smelled like dead fish. He alternated between growling and whining. Even a treat couldn't pacify him.

"It's a long time till morning," Dennis complained. "Are we just going to sit here and wait?"

"Do you have a better idea?" Ted barked. "Would a sing-along or a storytelling hour make you happy? If so, go hit up Snowden and see what he's up to."

Dennis clamped his lips shut and slumped down in his seat. He closed his eyes and tried to imagine what was to come. He opened his eyes to squint at the green numerals on his watch. The girls should be arriving anytime now. Hopefully, things would run true to form.

Once the women were on scene in any other mission, things started to happen faster than flying bullets. He wondered why that was. He made a mental note to ask Jack, who was an authority on all things women. He settled back, the soft murmurs of the others lulling him into a light sleep.

"What are you thinking, mate?" Fergus asked, poking Charles lightly on the arm.

"Nothing good, Ferg. Nothing good. I'm trying to wrap my brain around a man who would threaten to kill a priest. Dealing with someone like that is not something we have ever come up against. We have to assume that the men Avery calls wharf rats are just like him, and killing the villagers will be no big deal to them. We need to tread lightly here."

"When you say we, do you mean us, or are you including the women when they get here?"

Charles rubbed at the stubble on his cheeks and chin. Fergus could actually hear the rough scrape as his hands moved back and forth. "The women are fearless. And that's what worries me." Fergus nodded in agreement.

Both men turned silent as they listened to the rain slam on top of the van. It wasn't a soothing sound, more like subdued gunfire. "They're late, Ferg. They should have been here thirty minutes ago. I'm starting to worry."

Fergus nodded, but said, "Kathryn is an experienced driver. It's the rain, and these roads aren't like the smooth ones we have back in the States. They'll get here even if they have to crawl. You more than anyone should know that."

"I do, but that still doesn't stop me from worrying. It's not like them not to be calling with progress reports."

"They might be sleeping," Fergus said lamely.

Cyrus reared up and barked. He sprinted to the front of the van. He threw his head back and let loose with an unholy howl.

"I think the girls have just arrived, Charles. You were worried for nothing, mate."

"Open the door for him, Charles," Jack called from the back of the van.

Cyrus was through the door lightning fast. A bolt of thunder sounded, drowning out all other noise.

Charles's phone rang. He clicked it on. "We're here, dear. What do you suggest? We can't all fit in any van, so let's just talk until this rain lets up. Avery is here with us, as is Cyrus. First things first, how far are we from the village? Are we safe in this area? What's the plan at first light? Will we be visible?"

"A mile from the village, luv. We are as safe as we can be. If Araceli sends out a few of his men to check the area, that may change. The plan at first light is for Jack and Harry to head to the village and the rectory posing as members of a mountain-climbing club. Other members to arrive by midmorning. The back story is that two guides in the village, young boys, actually, agreed for a healthy fee to take the club up the mountain. The meeting place is to be the rectory. That's the plan. For now. What's up on your end?"

Myra explained what she knew about Annie's business manager and Abner and the money transfer. "All communication between Enrico and us is through Connor. They are stalling on the wire transfer until dawn. He said he wants Annie at the rectory to write the letter he's demanding. He wants it all done at once. We're stalling on that, too."

"All right, luv, sit tight. Are you keeping Cyrus, Jack wants to know."

Myra laughed. "Right now he's snuggling with Nikki, so yes, for now, he's with us." Her voice changed to a low, intimate level. "I can't wait to see you. I've really missed you, dear."

Charles was so choked up he nodded, until he realized Myra couldn't see him. "And I you, luv. Be careful."

"Always."

Fergus looked so crestfallen, Charles clapped him on the back. He was about to whisper some consoling words when his phone vibrated. He didn't think he'd ever seen his old friend move so fast. He turned away, a smile on his face, when he heard Fergus say, "Annie! Are you all right? God, I missed you. Will you marry me?"

The occupants of the van turned silent. Five minutes later, they asked as one, "What did she say?"

"She said she'll give it some serious thought. I'm thinking that's almost as good as a yes."

The gang hooted and hollered as they clapped Fergus on the back.

"If I had a flag, I'd run it up the flagpole. Annie never says anything she doesn't mean. Let's all think positive when she gets around to thinking seriously about your proposal."

Fergus leaned back in his seat, a sappy look on his face. He closed his eyes. Everyone suddenly knew what he was thinking. Annie walking down the aisle with Fergus, and the rest of them waiting at the altar.

The van went silent and remained that way until they heard Cyrus scratching at the door. Charles felt his eyes snap open. It was getting light out, and the rain had finally stopped. He opened the door. Cyrus raced to the back of the van and literally leaped onto Jack's lap, yipping and yapping the whole time. They tussled for a few minutes until Jack whistled for silence.

"Listen up, people. Not a good idea to congregate outside. A crowd like ours just begs to be noticed, so let's just stay in telephone contact. It's seven o'clock. At seven thirty, Harry and I will walk into the village and head straight for the rectory. I'll give whomever answers the door our spiel, and from there on in it's a crapshoot. We could be invited in and become prisoners. Or they could slam the door in our faces. Again, a crapshoot. We are taking Cyrus with us. My gut is telling me we'll become immediate prisoners. Any comments?" There were no comments.

"Annie is waiting for us to give her the signal to head to the village. It's going to take her a bit longer than it will take the two of you because of her injured knee. The girls are waiting to hear from Connor and Abner. The moment he's ready to do the wire transfer, she will start out. Forty minutes tops," Charles said.

"We need to do a check, Jack. What are you and Harry carrying with you in the way of ID," Fergus asked.

"We have to pick it up from Snowden, along with the gear he wants us to carry. He said he has some kind of machine that cranks out IDs that will pass muster. We belong to the Sierra Mountain Climbers. A bogus credit card along with a bogus Canadian driver's license. We are carrying euros and good old American money. Harry has Vietnamese currency and some euros as well. His driver's license will be from Vietnam. The Sierra Mountain Climbers is a worldwide organization, should the question come up. Our guides are supposed to be two young men from the village, brothers named Berto and Franko. Harry and I will be carrying burner phones that Snowden will have preprogrammed. There are seven of us making the climb. The other five are to arrive midmorning. We're to say we already paid the guides two thousand euros. We have a crumpled-up receipt to prove it. I think that covers it. All we have to do is pick up our mountain-climbing gear and the rest of the stuff."

Harry made his way to the front of the van,

Cyrus right behind him, with Jack bringing up the rear.

"Be careful, Jack," Dennis said.

"I will, Dennis. You take care, too."

Snowden was waiting for them and had everything ready. There was no conversation. The boys loaded up and waved airily as they started off, Cyrus in the lead.

"What do we do if this maniac asks where our vehicle is? No one mentioned that," Harry said.

"We had to leave it so the other climbers would know we're on the scene. They are waiting for us. It's thin as far as explanations go, but it should work. If not, oh, well! I wasn't expecting this cold," Jack said, hunkering into his shearling jacket.

"Wuss," Harry snapped.

Cyrus stopped and looked back at Harry to be sure he'd heard right. "Get over it, Cyrus." Harry grinned.

"One of these days, that dog is going to take a chunk out of your ass for insulting me," Jack said.

"What do you think I'll be doing while he's biting my ass?"

"Bleeding!" Jack guffawed. Cyrus yipped his agreement.

"Enough. I can see the village. What time is it?"

"Almost eight o'clock. We're on schedule. Do you see any activity?"

"Negative. Where's the rectory?"

"Snowden said it's the third building on the right. Brick. Small building, small porch. Big tree in the front yard. I can see it. You see it, Harry?"

"Yeah. Let's go for it!"

Cyrus fell back and walked alongside Jack. He was quivering with excitement.

"Easy, boy, easy."

"Okay, we're here," Jack said, walking up the three steps to the small porch. He stomped his feet to alert the people inside that there was company at the door. He pounded three short thumps with his closed fist.

The door was opened almost immediately by a young priest. His collar gleamed in the gloomy morning. "Can I help you?" he stammered.

"I hope so," Jack said cheerfully. "I'm sorry we're late, but the weather held us up. Are you Father Mendoza?"

"No, no, I'm Father Diaz. Why are you here?"

"To do the climb. Father Mendoza set it all up. We're to meet two brothers here at the rectory to take us up the mountain as soon as the other members get here. They should be here by midmorning. You look surprised, Father. Is there some sort of problem?" Jack asked, his voice sounding worried. "Are the guides here? Berto and Franco are their names. We already paid them two thousand euros."

"I . . . I don't know. Father Mendoza didn't tell me he was expecting anyone. I don't know anything about a mountain-climbing expedition."

Jack let impatience creep into his voice. "Well, then may I make a suggestion? Ask Father Mendoza. It's cold out here. Can we at least step inside until we straighten this out?"

The door was suddenly ripped wide open, and the young priest was yanked backward into the room. A tall man brandishing a gun appeared out of nowhere. Jack and Harry took a step backward; Cyrus did the same thing.

Jack's and Harry's hands immediately shot in the air. "Whoa, whoa! Look, we don't want any trouble. Keep the money. We'll do the climb without the guides. Sorry we bothered you."

"Shut up! Get in here, so we can give you your refund." The voice was a snarl, but it was the way the man held the gun that convinced Jack and Harry to do his bidding. Cyrus trotted along next to Jack, his ears straight up, his tail tucked between his legs.

"What's going on?" Harry squeaked, his face full of panic.

"I told you to shut up. Get over there at the table and sit down. Keep that dog quiet, or I'll shoot him."

Cyrus knew a threat when he heard one. He immediately dropped to his belly at Jack's feet.

"Who are you? What are you doing here?"

"I told you. We're mountain climbers. We belong to a club. Father Mendoza arranged two guides to take our small club up the mountain. That's what we do on our vacation. We heard about this mountain owned by the de Silva family. The information we had said the family was royalty and some count owned it now, but that it was abandoned. We wanted to check it out. Why are you holding a gun? You can keep the two thousand euros. Just let us go. We'll find another mountain to climb. Where's Father Mendoza?"

"I'm over here, my son. I'm sorry for this poor reception. I didn't mean for this to happen."

"What is happening, Father? We don't understand."

"I ask the questions. Who are you?" Enrico demanded again.

"I just told you who we are. We're just normal people on vacation who just happen to be mountain climbers. There is nothing else I can tell you."

"I don't believe you. Who sent you here? Empty your pockets and put everything on the table."

"The main chapter of our group. They found this place, and we jumped on it. More to the point, who are you?" Jack asked boldly, as he and Harry emptied their pockets.

"I'm the guy with the gun. Just sit there and be quiet. Make a move, and I'll shoot the old priest, then the dog. No talking."

Enrico walked away to where Father Mendoza was sitting at his desk. He looked down at his phone and saw that an incoming call was from Connor. Once again, there were no amenities. Connor got right to the point. "The wire transfer will be ready to go in thirty minutes. I've just heard from the countess. She is on her way to you. She gave me instructions to wait to do the transfer until she is in your company. Call me when she arrives, and we'll make the transfer."

Enrico was about to chastise the financial wizard but realized he would be talking to dead air.

It was happening. He'd done it. Finally. Enrico grew so light-headed, he thought he was going to black out. He gave his head a shake to clear it. He looked down at the phone and punched in his brother's number. "Mateo, come up here to the rectory. Has the guard returned?"

"Why? No, he has not returned."

"Because I said so. There has been an unforeseen situation, and I need you. Quickly, Mateo, or you'll regret it for the rest of your life."

"Hey, you with the gun, what's going on here? Come on, man. Let us get on with our climb. We're out a lot of money here, man?" Jack yelled across the room.

"It's not your concern. Father," he said to the young priest, "fetch me the things on the table. Frisk them, and do not be shy about it. Move!" Enrico bellowed.

"Stand up, señor," Father Diaz said gently, as he ran his hands up and down Jack's body. Jack whispered, hoping the priest wasn't too panicked to listen to him.

"We're the good guys, Father. We're here to help you. Annie sent us." The young priest stumbled but righted himself as he moved over to Harry.

"There are no weapons," he called out. Father Diaz gathered up the ID cards, the cell phones, and the money. He carried it all back and dropped it on the old priest's desk. Enrico picked up the cards and looked at them carefully.

"These look new."

"That's because they are new. Look at the renewal date. We just got new cards two weeks ago. What's going on here? Who the hell are you?"

"No one you want to know. These are cheap phones."

"And what? You think we're going to carry seven-hundred-dollar smartphones up a mountain where there is no cell tower? Maybe you think we look like fools, but we aren't. We just follow our leader's instructions, which were to use a local cell phone. You got a problem with that, take it up with our leader.

"I'm going to ask you again, what's going on here? This is kidnapping because you are holding us against our will."

Enrico shrugged. "You need to shut up if you ever want to climb another mountain. This will all be over shortly. It will either end peacefully or not. Your future depends on how smoothly things go."

Enrico walked to the door just as the others in the room heard a loud pounding. He raised the locking bar and opened the door. A rough-looking man entered the room, his gaze raking the room. "Who are these people?"

"If you believe them, they're mountain climbers. I do not believe them. I want you to guard them because I don't trust them. The countess is on her way. Do you understand what I just said, Mateo?"

"I'm not deaf. Why did you tie up the constable and his deputy? There's no need for that."

"Are you questioning me, brother? They had guns, that's why they're tied up. Where is your gun?"

Mateo turned around and yanked up his jacket. No need to tell him the gun was empty.

"Do you have anything else to report?"

Mateo snorted. "It stopped raining. It's very cold outside. There's no heat in the church or the schoolhouse. No one knows how to work these old-fashioned units."

"And I should care about that, why?"

"Because there are old people, children, and two babies who need to be warm. Is that enough of a reason?"

"You're a bleeding heart just like your brother."

Mateo was saved from a response when a loud knocking could be heard.

Enrico's eyes sparked like stars on a Christmas tree.

At last.

The countess had come through just the way he knew she would.

Chapter 15

Annie took in the room with one sweeping gaze before she limped her way to the desk, where the old priest was sitting, his expression miserable. She ignored Enrico and said, "I am so sorry for all of this, Padre. I'm trying to make it right. Just tell me you're all right, that you haven't been mistreated by this cretin."

"I'm fine, Countess," the old priest whispered harshly. His head bobbed up and down to confirm his words.

Annie whirled around to face Enrico. "Well? You called this meeting, so I suggest you gavel it to order so we can be done with this."

Enrico's eyes narrowed. "Are those my clothes you're wearing?"

"Sad to say, they are. And may I say you have terrible taste. This cashmere is very low grade.

It makes me itch. In other words, you can't make a silk purse out of a sow's ear. All the cashmere in the world can't make you into something you're not. Oh, and I took a shower while I was at your fancy pimp digs, and I ate your food and drank your wine. Even the wine was inferior. But when in Rome . . ."

Annie looked around. "Who are these people?" she asked, pointing to Jack and Harry?

"Your talents as an actress leave a lot to be desired. Don't pretend you don't know them. They're your people, sent here to try to take me down. You're all such fools."

Annie walked over to where Jack and Harry were sitting. She bent down to look at them, her expression blank. She turned around, yanking at the cashmere top to straighten it around her hips. Directly in front of Jack, she said, "No, I don't recognize either one of these men, or that one standing over there by the constable." She almost blacked out when she felt the gun in her waistband being removed by Jack. She gave the shirt another hitch as she made her way back to where the two priests waited.

"Not that it's any of your business, but the other man is my brother. You lie. They lie. Take a good look at them. Do they look like mountain climbers? You don't climb a mountain wearing sneakers. Look at their hands, there are no calluses. Do you take me for a fool?"

Annie shrugged. "If the shoe fits . . . I never saw either one of those men. Are we going to get to it, or are we going to stand here trading insults? But, before I okay the transfer, I want proof that the villagers are safe. Release them first."

"Don't tell me what to do. I give the orders here. The villagers will be released when our business is finished."

Annie squared her shoulders and tried to stand tall, but her knee was throbbing so badly, she thought her leg would give out on her. "No, first you release them. What? Are you going to shoot me? I don't think so. You need me."

"That's true. But I don't need this old man praying on his beads. And I don't need the young one, who looks like he's going to faint any minute. Now, can we get down to business?"

Annie looked at the two frightened priests and knew that she was beaten. She turned around and made eye contact with Enrico's brother. He stared at her, a helpless expression on his face. No help there. She risked a glance at Harry, who stared back at her, his expression blank.

"Hey, lady, will you just do what that guy wants you to do so we can get out of here? We have people waiting for us, and a mountain to climb. We're on vacation, and all we're doing is wasting time. Plus, if you don't get on with this, we're going to be out two thousand euros," Jack called out.

"Mateo, shut that fool up. Gag him. I'm sick of his mouth. Make the call, Countess."

"Yeah, Mateo, shut me up!" Jack taunted.

Cyrus barked, his head snapping up as he got to his feet.

"Someone is coming," Mateo said as he craned his neck to look out the window next to the heavy front door. "Five men!"

"The rest of our group!" Jack shouted. "I told you, but you wouldn't listen."

Cyrus continued to bark, the sound loud and shrill.

The fierce pounding on the door thundered in the room. Enrico motioned for the young priest to open the door. "Mateo, get over here; I want you at my side."

"Go," Jack hissed. "We have your back. We know you aren't part of this."

Mateo's eyes popped wide at what he was hearing. Jack gave a slight nod as all hell broke loose when the boys moved into the already crowded rectory. Enrico fired the gun in his hand, two quick bursts of firepower. One shot went wild, the other hit the constable in the shoulder. A blossom of blood appeared on his white shirt. Stunned, his face turned white.

Enrico fired again, into the ceiling. "Quiet!" he roared. The room went silent. Cyrus stopped barking, not because of Enrico's order but because of Jack's touch to his head.

"Not yet, buddy, but soon. Easy, boy." Cyrus trembled with excitement.

"Everyone, move to the kitchen. Sit down on the floor with your legs out in front of you. The first one who opens his mouth or makes a false move will be shot. I only give one warning."

"Please, gentlemen, do as he says," the old priest pleaded.

"You're insane, Enrico," Annie said as she watched Charles and the others do as ordered.

"Move!" Enrico said to the old priest. He gave him a vicious shove. Father Mendoza fell from his chair as the young priest ran to help him. He pulled him out of the way, so Annie could take his seat at the desk to use the computer. A tear trickled down her cheek.

"Type the newspaper release that I prepared. I want it to hit the airwaves when the money transfer occurs. It will go out to every newspaper in Spain, and the wire services will pick it up and it will be global. I've waited a lifetime for this. Now, do it!"

Annie started to type. Then she burst into laughter. "You can't be serious! No one is going to print this! They'll think this is a joke. The world doesn't care that I am saying you are my dead husband's legitimate heir and that you are assuming the title of count as his successor."

Blind rage rushed through Enrico. He pressed the gun to Annie's head to encourage her to type faster. She did.

When she was finished, she leaned back in her chair. "Now what?"

"Now you hit SEND and send it out to all the papers on the list." Annie did as instructed.

"Satisfied?"

"Yes, now call Connor and arrange for the wire transfer."

Again, Annie did as instructed. She waited for the call to go through. Cyrus barked; then the door burst open. Annie dropped the phone but picked it up in time to hear Connor say, "I'm doing it as we speak. Stand by."

Enrico didn't know where to look, at the computer or at the gaggle of women who were suddenly crowding into the room. His eyes almost popped out of his head when he saw Myra at the same moment he saw the blizzard of numbers lock into place, turning him into an instant billionaire. Then the screen went blank.

"Control those women, Mateo. Shoot the first one who makes a move." Hysterical excitement rang in his voice.

"What the hell did you do, Countess? Connor, what are you trying to do? The money disappeared. You better have a satisfactory answer, or I'm going to spray this room with bullets!" To prove his point, Enrico let loose with a volley of shots that ricocheted around the room.

"Listen to me, you idiot! The transfer went through. You saw it! If something is wrong, it's on your end, not here. I'm sending you the confirmation. From here on in, this is your problem." Annie craned her neck to see the confirmation that appeared on the screen in front of her.

Enrico leaned forward. It was just as Connor said. He knew a confirmation when he saw one. Connor had upheld his end of the bargain. What to do? He looked around at the gaggle of people who seemed to be frozen in place. Somehow, some way, the countess had outsmarted him. And yet, he'd seen the money.

"Look! Here it is!" Annie said.

Enrico felt his heart skip a beat as he stared down at the long line of numbers. It was there. The money really was in his account. He felt light-headed with relief. Now came the good part. The part where he moved the money to other accounts around the world. But before he did that, he had to deal with the business at hand.

"We're done here. I did everything you wanted. Let the villagers go. The constable needs a doctor. The padre has a gash on his head that needs tending to. Before you go, though, I want my belongings back. And my friend wants hers back, too. Like now would be good," Annie drawled as she let her gaze rake over the girls, then to the boys. "*Now*, Enrico!"

Cyrus knew what *now* meant. He moved, a black streak soaring through the air to land on Enrico's back. The force of his lunge threw Enrico across the desk. Just as Cyrus sunk his teeth into Enrico's backside, Annie scooped up the gun that had slid across the shiny surface of the priest's desk. The room erupted in sound as seven women moved as one.

Mateo threw his hands in the air in a sign of surrender. Alexis pinned him against the wall, relieving him of his gun. "It's not loaded."

"I know." Alexis grinned. "Not to worry, we know you're on the padre's side. Just stay out of the way, okay?"

Mateo nodded. Mother of God, who were these people?

"Hold, Cyrus!" Annie said. She risked a glance at the big dog and almost laughed out loud at the firm grip he had on Enrico's rear end. It didn't look like he was *ever* going to let go.

"Okay, cowboy, this is what you're going to do. You are going to call those wharf rats of yours and tell them to release the villagers and to come here ASAP. I know there's a doctor and a nurse somewhere in the village. Tell them to send them here to take care of the constable. Do it, you son of a bitch, or this dog is going to work his way around to your royal jewels. If you screw this up, I *will* shoot you."

"If he won't do it, I will," Mateo shouted.

"Traitor!" Enrico thundered, but he reached for his phone to do what Annie had instructed.

"Ten minutes, people. Spread out. Wait for all of them to get inside before you attack. Remember, they all have guns. Boys, go out the back door and be ready to follow the rats once they get inside. You need to cover our backs. Go!" Annie barked.

"Annie, where are our belongings? Did he bring them with him?" Myra shouted.

"He has a rucksack somewhere. I saw it earlier. It's heavy-duty black nylon."

Kathryn rushed forward. "You need to sit down, Annie. You're looking pale," she whispered. Annie nodded and relinquished the gun in her hand to Kathryn.

"Found it!" Myra shouted happily. She immediately started to paw through the contents. "Eeew, I hate touching anything that belongs to him."

"How do you think I feel, and I'm wearing his clothes," Annie quipped.

"It's all here, our special phones, our gold badges, and our passports. Do we want the rest of his junk?"

"Separate it, but take it. We might need it later," Nikki said.

"Where's Snowden?" Maggie asked.

"Outside somewhere. He's got eyes on the school, the church, and the houses that some of the villagers are stuck in. I heard Charles talking to him, that's how I know," Kathryn said.

"Get this damn dog off me before I bleed to death," Enrico bellowed.

"Tell that to someone who cares. We-do-not-care-if-you-bleed-to-death," Nikki said. "Hold, Cyrus!"

"Here come the wharf rats," Yoko said from her position by the window. "I have to say, they are a scary-looking crew."

"Quick, stand in front of this sack of pus so when they come through the door, they don't see him and the dog so lovingly attached to his rear end," Nikki ordered.

The girls scurried to do her bidding. Yoko stayed by the window and was the one who opened the door.

"You make a sound, Enrico, and it will be your last," Myra hissed in Enrico's ear.

The moment the door closed behind the

wharf rats, the girls went into action. The melee took less than five minutes. The only ones who broke a sweat were the wharf rats they had trussed up like Thanksgiving turkeys.

The two priests, eyes wide, were speechless with what was happening in their little house, which had never seen excitement of any kind, much less what had just happened. They were so excited they forgot to finger the beads that were always in their hands. It was a good thing, Annie thought. Well, sort of, she corrected the thought.

A knock on the door sounded. Yoko, the closest, opened it to admit the village doctor and his nurse. Right on their heels, the boys barreled through the door, took in the situation, and moved forward.

"Release, Cyrus. Good boy!" Cyrus backed away, quivering with excitement. He loved the praise. He then moved forward to stare at Enrico, who drew back in horror when Cyrus bared his teeth and growled.

"Get that damn devil dog away from me! I need a doctor."

"I need a good cold beer, but I doubt there's one here in the rectory, so that means if I don't get what I want, your chances of getting what you want are slim to none. In other words, you get a doctor when he's finished taking care of the constable. Of course, if he opts not to treat you, that's on you. So shut up, or Cyrus will go for the jewels. Your call."

Enrico looked over at his brother. "Traitor. I can't believe you betrayed me. I'm your brother! We're family. You were supposed to have my back. Where's Flavio, or did he turn on me, too?"

Mateo turned his back on Enrico and walked outside to where his brother was smoking a cigarette. "Can we leave now?"

"I don't think anyone will miss us if we just walk away," Mateo said sadly. "How did this happen, Flavio? How?"

Flavio shrugged. "He was just a brother in name only. If I never see or hear of him again, it won't bother me. I'm ready to go home, so let's go."

"It's a long walk, brother."

"I don't care; I'll crawl if I have to. I need to wash this evil off me."

Jack watched the two brothers as they walked away. He walked outside and whistled sharply to gain the brothers' attention. They turned immediately to stare at him. Jack fired off a sloppy salute of thanks. The brothers did the same thing.

Avery Snowden's oversize van pulled up in front of the rectory. He stepped out, his operatives right behind him. Inside the rectory, Charles pointed to the trussed-up wharf rats. "The girls made it easy for you. We don't ever want these creatures to come back here to terrorize the padres and the villagers. You can do whatever you want with Enrico."

"He's bleeding," Snowden said.

"Yes, I saw that," Charles conceded.

"You gonna have the doc patch him up, or do we take him as is?"

"Just get him out of here," Charles responded.

Enrico roared his protest. Cyrus raced over to the man and rose on his hind legs to eyeball Enrico. Enrico sagged, and said, "Okay, okay, just get me out of here." Cyrus barked happily. The shepherd was adding up the treats he was due and looking forward to receiving his payment.

When the door closed behind the constable, who was leaning heavily on the doctor, the room went totally quiet. It was the young priest who finally broke the silence. "Thank you for coming to our aid. We"—he motioned to Padre Mendoza—"apologize for our lack of help. We hope you understand. Is the village safe now?"

"Everything is fine now, Father," Annie said. "No one will bother you ever again. You can all go back to your uneventful bucolic lives, with my personal apology for invading your peace and quiet. I don't have the words to tell you how sorry I am that all of you had to go through all this."

"It's not your fault, Countess. Just know you have our thanks."

"I think it's time for us to leave," Kathryn said.

Hands were shaken, hugs were tight, and smiles were wide before everyone trooped outside.

"Time to go home," Nikki said.

"Not yet," Myra said. "I have to go to the mountaintop. I want to gather up my pearls. Just so you know, I'm not leaving without my pearls. And I have another stop I have to make. I need to go to a bank and find a packaging store so I can return Astrid's hat and the rest of her belongings. There is no way that I'm leaving this country until I make things right with that young woman."

"We'll help you," Nikki said happily. "We'll head to the airport, helicopter in, and get the pearls; then we'll help you with your English fairy godmother. And then we'll all head home."

"No. No, we're not going home. We're going to—" Annie said.

"Vegas!" the gang shouted as one.

With that declaration, Fergus scooped up Annie and headed for the van.

Annie sighed with happiness despite the throbbing pain in her leg.

"I missed you, Fergus. I thought I might never see you again. I didn't like the feeling. Fergus . . . I . . . want to . . . to change my name."

Fergus stopped in his tracks. He looked down at Annie. "Do you just want to change your name because you can do that legally, or do you want to change your name to Duffy?" He held his breath as he waited for Annie's reply.

Annie merely smiled.

Epilogue

Three months later

It was a blustery day in mid-March, with light snow falling, when the Sisters gathered in Myra's kitchen at Pinewood. A monster fire burned in the old fieldstone fireplace, adding to the warmth of the old farmhouse. The girls loved a good, cozy fire, especially Myra.

Tantalizing aromas wafted through the entire house, cinnamon, possibly baked apples, Charles would neither confirm nor deny, and the heavenly scent of some kind of soup that would, they all knew, be robust and served with hot, crusty bread lathered with melted butter.

Maggie and Kathryn were salivating as Charles shooed them away from his stove.

"I don't get it. Since when does Avery Snowden get to call a meeting?" Nikki asked as she stretched her neck, hoping to get a glimpse of what was in the oven. Baked apples or apple pie?

Charles held both hands up in the air. "He asked politely. He's just back from England on a project for MI6. He made a side trip to Spain to attend a wedding and said he had information he wanted to share with us. How could I refuse?"

"We see your point, dear. I guess our question is, since he called this meeting, where is he? You called the meeting for noon, and it's now three o'clock. The dinner hour is approaching."

"I have no idea, Myra. It is snowing out."

Kathryn said something everyone pretended not to hear. Lady reared up at the same moment and trotted over to the door, her pups on her heels.

"I think he's finally here," Nikki said.

Avery blew into the kitchen like a gust of wind. Everyone started talking at once, then waited as Snowden tussled with Lady and handed out treats to her and her pups.

"Smells delicious in here," he said, grinning from ear to ear.

"You're welcome to stay for supper," Charles said magnanimously.

"I'd be a fool to turn down one of your gourmet suppers, Sir Charles. So, shall we get to it?"

"That's why we're all here." He turned around and motioned for the others to follow him down to the war room, where Lady Justice presided to conduct business. The group saluted her as one before they took their seats at the table. Charles called the meeting to order. "You have the floor, Avery. Before you take it, though, what's that buzzing sound coming from your vest?"

Snowden laughed out loud. The women looked at one another as they tried to figure out if they'd ever heard the old spy laugh. They waited as he opened his vest to allow a small head to peek out at the group. "This is Happy. I found her when we were in Spain. She's my roommate. I tried to find her owner, but no one had a missing pet, so I couldn't leave her behind. He continued to smile as the Sisters ooohed and aaaahed over the little animal, who purred contentedly as she enjoyed all the attention.

"Can we get on with it, Avery?"

"Absolutely, Sir Charles. I really wanted to get out here sooner, but I had other commitments, but I'm here now. After I finished up my business with MI6, I traveled to Spain to attend a double wedding. Yes, Enrico's brothers both got married and relocated to the Village of Tears, where they will put down roots. The villagers welcomed them with open arms once Father Mendoza explained the situation to them. In fact, the priest gave each of them a plot of land, and plans are under way for the villagers to help build their houses.

"I . . . ah . . . convinced Enrico to sign over all his bank accounts and property to his brothers. He . . . um . . . balked at first, but finally he came around to my way of thinking.

The brothers will use the money wisely for themselves and the villagers. We managed to sell Enrico's Ferrari, and they bought two mini-vans and a truck. Oh, and, Annie, the three trucks that you ordered for the village were finally delivered, and produce is being shipped on schedule. When I said goodbye, the whole village turned out to wish me well.

"Myra, Sophia wanted me to tell you that the young lady from whom you obtained much-needed help at the airport appeared some time after the Christmas holiday. She works as a secretary at an exclusive children's academy in London. She wanted to personally thank the person who returned her hat and other belongings, along with the extremely generous check that she said would take care of her for the rest of her life."

Myra smiled, then frowned. "But, Avery, how did she know where to go to try and find me?"

"The packaging store you used is across the street from the Internet café that Dr. Miguel used. The store's address was the return address on the package, so she went there first. Sophia was hazy as to why and how the young lady went to the café, but somehow she homed in on Dr. Miguel, who, I assume, told her what she needed to know. You made one young lady very happy, Myra."

Myra nodded as she fingered the pearls at her neck. "You found your pearls!" Avery said.

"We found forty-seven out of sixty. Charles had them strung for me. I have to say I feel whole again," Myra said happily.

Snowden smacked his hands together, a silly grin on his face. He handed over a flash drive to Charles. "This is from Sophia and Dr. Miguel, and it's for Annie."

"What is it, what is it?" the girls demanded, excitement ringing in their voices.

"Watch!" was all Snowden said by way of explanation.

Lady Justice faded to reveal Dr. Andres Miguel dressed in his white doctor's coat, a stethoscope hanging around his neck, standing next to Sophia, who wore a similar coat. Both were smiling, the sun behind them. The doctor spoke.

"Countess, I don't have the words to thank you for all of this," the doctor said, waving his hands behind him. "In my wildest dreams, I never ever thought we here in this little province would have such a high-tech medical facility. An MRI machine! I have doctors and nurses begging me to let them come here to work. But most important, our patients are the recipients of your kindness. Lives will be saved, thanks to you. I wish there was something more Sophia and I could say besides thank you. For now it is the best we can do.

"We even have two ambulances. Sophia sold her little cottage, I sold my house, and we purchased an apartment here within walking distance of the clinic. So, thank you again.

"And now we want you to see the sign over the clinic. The man behind the camera zoomed in on the monster letters over the entrance to the clinic. "The name lights up at night, so people can see it and know where to come for help."

Annie bit down on her lower lip, tears pooling in her eyes.

THE ELENA DE SILVA MEDICAL CENTER

Myra hugged Annie as the girls leaped up to do the same thing. The tears continued to roll down Annie's cheeks.

"Is this where you quote Picasso again," Nikki whispered.

"'The meaning of life is to find your gift. The purpose of life is to give it away,'" Annie whispered in return. The smile that accompanied her words rivaled the sun.

*See how it all began with a special new edition of
the very first book in Fern Michaels bestselling and
beloved Sisterhood series . . .*

WEEKEND WARRIORS

Life isn't fair. Most women know it. But what
can you do about it? Plenty . . . if you're part
of the Sisterhood. On the surface, these seven
women are as different as can be—but each
has had her share of bad luck, from cheating
husbands to sexist colleagues to a legal system
that often doesn't do its job. Now, drawn
together by tragedy, they're forging a bond that
will help them right the wrongs committed
against them and discover an inner strength
they didn't know they had. Growing bolder
with each act of justice, the Sisterhood is
learning that when bad things happen, you
can roll over and play dead . . . or you can get
up fighting. . . .

*Includes special bonus material celebrating
the Sisterhood series!
A Zebra mass-market paperback and
eBook on sale now.
Keep reading for a special look!*

Washington, D.C.

The traffic was horrendous on Massachusetts Avenue, but then it was always horrendous at this time of day. Rush hour. God, how she hated those words. Especially today. She slapped the palm of her hand on the horn and muttered under her breath, "C'mon you jerk, move!"

"Take it easy, Nik," Barbara Rutledge said, her eyes on the slow moving traffic. "One more block and we're there. Mom won't mind if we're a few minutes late. She hates it that she turned sixty today so the longer she has to wait for the celebration, the better she'll feel. I don't think she looks sixty, do you Nik?"

"Are you kidding! She looks better than we do and we're only thirty-six." She leaned on the horn again even though it was an exercise in futility. "Just tell me one thing, why did your mother pick the Jockey Club for dinner?"

"The first crab cakes of the season, that's why. President Reagan made this restaurant famous and all her political friends come here. If you want my opinion, thirty bucks for two crab cakes is obscene. I can eat lunch all week on thirty bucks if I'm careful. Mom pitched a fit last week when I took her to Taco Bell for lunch. We both ate for five bucks. She was a good sport about it but she can't understand why I don't tap into the trust fund. I keep telling her I want to make it on my own. Some days she understands, some days she doesn't. I know she's proud of me, you, too, Nik. She tells everyone about her two crime fighting girls who are lawyers."

"I love her as much as you do, Barb. I can't imagine growing up without a mother. I would have if she hadn't stepped in and taken over when my parents died. Okay, we're here and we're only thirty minutes late. This isn't the best parking spot in the world but it will have to do and we're under a streetlight. In this city it doesn't get any better than that."

"We really should hit the powder room before we head for the table. Mom does like spit and polish, not to mention perfume and lipstick," Barbara said, trying to smooth the wrinkles out of her suit. Nik did the same thing.

"I spent the day in court and so did you. We're supposed to look wrinkled, messy and harried. Myra will understand. Oops, almost forgot my present," Nik said, reaching into the backseat for a small silver-wrapped package. She handed Barbara a long cylinder tied with a bright red ribbon. "Your brain must be as tired as mine. You almost forgot yours, too. What about this pile of books, Barb?"

"They're for Mom. I picked them up today at lunchtime. You know how she loves reading about murder and mayhem. I'll give them to her when we leave."

Myra Rutledge was waiting, a beautiful woman whose smile and open arms welcomed them. "My girls are here. We're ready to be seated now, Franklin," Myra said.

"Certainly, madam. Your usual table, or would you prefer the smoking section with a window view?"

"The window, Franklin," Barbara said. "I think tonight in honor of my mother's birthday you two can have a cigarette. Just one cigarette after dinner for both of you. I will of course abstain. Yes, yes, yes, I know we all quit but this is Mom's birthday and I say why not."

Myra smiled as she reached for her daughter's hand. "Why not indeed."

"This is so wonderful," Myra said, sitting down and leaning across the table. "My two favorite girls. I couldn't ask for a better finale to my birthday."

"Finale, Mom! Does that mean when you go home, you and Charles won't celebrate?"

"Well . . . I . . . perhaps a glass of sherry. I did ask Charles to come but he said this was a mother daughter dinner and he would feel out of place. No comments, girls."

"Mom, when are you going to marry the guy? You've been together for twenty years. Nik and I know all about the birds and the bees so stop blushing," Barbara teased.

"Yes and it was Charles who told you two about the birds and the bees," Myra smiled.

Charles Emery was Myra's companion slash houseman. When his cover was blown as an MI6 agent his government had relocated him to the United States where he'd signed on as head of security for Myra's Fortune 500 candy business. His sole goal in life was to take care of Myra, a job he took seriously and did well. Both girls were grateful for his attention to Myra, lessening her loneliness when they went off on their own.

Myra's eyes sparkled. "Now, tell me everything. Your latest cases, who you're dating at the moment, how our softball team is doing. Don't leave anything out. Will I be planning a wedding any time soon?"

It was what Nikki loved about Myra the most, her genuine interest in their lives. She'd never invaded their privacy, always content to stand on the sidelines, offer motherly support and aid when needed but she never interfered, or gave advice unless asked. Nikki knew Myra enjoyed the times the three of them spent together, loved the twice-monthly dinners in town and the occasional lunches with her daughter or perhaps a short stroll along the Tidal Basin.

Yes, Myra had a life, a busy life, a life of her own beyond her girls. She sat on various charitable boards, worked tirelessly for both political parties, did numerous good deeds every day, was active in the Historical Society and still managed to have time for Charles, Barbara and herself.

"You staying in town tonight, Mom?"

A rosy hue marched across Myra's face. "No, Barbara, I'm going home. No, I didn't drive myself. I took a car service so don't fret about the trip to McLean. Charles is waiting for me. I told you, we'll have a glass of sherry together."

"No birthday cake!" Nik said.

The rosy hue crept down Myra's neck. "We had the cake at lunchtime. Charles needed a blowtorch to light all the candles. All sixty of them. It was very . . . festive."

"How does it feel to be sixty, Mom?" Barbara asked reaching for her mother's hand across the table. "You told me you were dreading the day."

"It's just a number, just a day. I don't feel any different than I did yesterday. People always talk about 'the moments' in their lives. The special times they never forget. I guess this day is one of those moments. The day I married your father was a special moment. The day you were born was an extra special moment, the day Nikki came to us was another special moment and then of course when the candy company went 500. Don't laugh at me now when I tell you the other special moment was when Charles said he would take care of me for the rest of my life. All wonderful moments. I hope I have years and years of special moments. If you would get married and give me a grandchild I would run up the flag, Barbara. I don't want to be so old I dodder when you give birth."

Nikki poked Barbara's arm, a huge smile on her face. "Go on, tell her. Make your mother happy on her sixtieth birthday."

"I'm pregnant, Mom. You can start planning the wedding, but you better make it quick or I'll be showing before you know it."

Myra looked first at Nikki to see if they were teasing her or not. Nikki's head bobbed up and down. "I'm going to be the maid of honor and the godmother! She's not teasing, Myra."

"Oh, honey. Are you happy? Of course you are. All I have to do is look at you. Oh, there is so much to do. You want the reception at home in the garden, right?"

"Absolutely, Mom. I want to be married in the living room. I want to slide down the bannister in my wedding gown. I'm going to do that, Mom. Nik will be right behind me. If I can't do that, the wedding is off."

"Anything you want, honey. Anything. You have made me the happiest woman in the whole world. Promise that you will allow Charles and me to babysit."

"She promised me first," Nikki grinned.

"This is definitely 'a moment.' Do either of you have a camera?"

"Mom, a camera is not something I carry around in my purse. However, all is not lost. Nik has one in her car. I'll scoot over there and get it."

Nikki fished in her pocket and tossed her the keys.

"I'm going to be a mother. Me! Do you believe it? You'll be Auntie Nik," Barbara said, bending over to tweak Nikki's cheek. I'll ask Franklin to take our picture when I get back. See ya," she said flashing them both an ear-to-ear grin.

"I hope you had a good day, today, Myra. Birthdays are always special," Nikki said, her gaze on the window opposite her chair. "Knowing you're going to be a grandmother has to be the most wonderful thing in the world. I'm pretty excited myself." She could see Barbara running across the street, her jacket flapping in the spring breeze. "Do you remember the time Barbara and I made you a birthday cake out of cornflakes, crackers and pancake syrup?"

"I'll never forget it. I don't think the cook ever forgot it either. I did eat it, though."

Nikki laughed. "Yes, you did." She was glad now she had parked under the streetlight. She could see several couples walking down the street, saw Barbara open the back door of the car, saw her reach for the camera, saw her sling it over her shoulder, saw her lock the door. She turned her attention to Myra, who was also staring out the window. Nikki's gaze swiveled back to the window to see Barbara look both ways for oncoming traffic, ready to sprint across the street at the first break. The three couples were almost upon her when she stepped off the curb.

Nikki was aware of the dark car that came out of nowhere, the sound of horns blowing and the sudden screech of brakes. Myra was moving off her seat almost in slow motion, her face a mask of disbelief as they both ran out of the restaurant. The scream when it came was so tortured, so animal-like, Nikki stopped in her tracks to reach for Myra's arm.

The awkward position of her friend's body was a picture that would stay with Nikki forever. She bent down, afraid to touch her friend, the friend she called sister. "Did anyone call an ambulance?" she shouted.

She heard a loud, jittery response. "Yes."

"No! No! No!" Myra screamed over and over as she dropped to the ground to cradle her daughter's body in her arms. From somewhere off in the distance, a siren could be heard. Nikki's trembling fingers fumbled for a pulse. Her whole body started to shake when she couldn't find even a faint beat. Maybe she wasn't doing it right. She pressed harder with her third and fourth fingers the way she'd seen nurses do. A wave of dizziness riveted through her just as the ambulance crew hit the ground running. Tears burned her eyes as she watched the paramedics check Barbara's vital signs.

Time lost all meaning as the medical crew did what they were trained to do. A young woman with long curly hair raised her head to look straight at Nikki. Her eyes were sad when she shook her head.

It couldn't be. She wanted to shout, to scream, to stamp her feet. Instead, she knuckled her eyes and stifled her sobs.

"She'll be all right, won't she Nikki? Broken

bones heal. She was just knocked unconscious. Tell me she'll be all right. Please, tell me that. Please, Nikki."

The lump in Nikki's throat was so large she thought she would choke. She tried not to look at the still body, tried not to see them straighten out Barbara's arms and legs. When they lifted her onto the stretcher, she closed her eyes. She thought she would lose it when the young woman with the long curly hair pulled a sheet up over her best friend's face. Not Barbara. Not her best friend in the whole world. Not the girl she played with in a sandbox, gone to kindergarten with. Not the girl she'd gone through high school, college and law school with. She was going to be her maid of honor, babysit her baby. How could she be dead? "I saw her look both ways before she stepped onto the curb. She had a clear path to cross the street," she mumbled.

"Nikki, should we ride in the ambulance with Barbara? Will they let us?" Myra asked tearfully.

She doesn't know. She doesn't know what the sheet means. How was she going to tell Myra her daughter was dead?

The ambulance doors closed. It drove off. The siren silent.

"It's too late. They left. You'll have to drive, Nikki. They'll need all sorts of information when they admit her to the hospital. I want to be there. Barbara needs to know I'm there.

She needs to know her mother is there. Can we go now, Nikki?" Myra pleaded.

"Ma'am?"

"Yes, officer," Nikki said. She loosened her hold on Myra's shoulders.

His voice was not unkind. He was too young to be this kind. She could see the compassion on his face.

"I need to take a statement. You are . . ."

"Nicole Quinn. This is Myra Rutledge. She's the mother . . ." She almost said, "of the deceased," but bit her tongue in time.

"Officer, can we do this later?" Myra interjected. "I have to get to the hospital. There will be so much paperwork to take care of. Do you know which hospital they took my daughter to? Was it George Washington or Georgetown Hospital?" Myra begged. Tears rolled down her wrinkled cheeks.

Nikki looked away. She knew she was being cowardly, but there was just no way she could get the words past her lips to tell Myra her only daughter was dead. She watched as police officers dispersed the crowd of onlookers until only the three couples remained. Where was the car that hit Barbara? Did they take it away already? Where was the driver? She wanted to voice the questions aloud but remained silent because of Myra.

Nikki watched as the young officer steeled himself for what he had to do. He worked his thin neck around the starched collar of his shirt, cleared his throat once, and then again.

"Ma'am, your daughter was taken to the morgue at George Washington Hospital. There's no hurry on the paperwork. I can have one of the officers take you to the hospital if you like. I'm . . . I'm sorry for your loss, ma'am."

Myra's scream was primal as she slipped to the ground. The young cop dropped to his knees. "I thought she knew. I didn't . . . Jesus . . ."

"We need to get her to a doctor right away. Will you stay with her for a minute, officer? I need to get my cell phone out of the car to make some calls." Her first call was to Myra's doctor and then she called Charles. Both promised to meet her at the emergency entrance to GW Hospital.

When she returned, Myra was sitting up, supported by the young officer. She looked dazed and her speech was incoherent. "She doesn't weigh much. I can easily carry her to the cruiser," the officer said. Nikki nodded gratefully.

"Can you tell me what happened, officer? Did you get the car that hit Barbara? Those couples standing over there must have seen everything. We even saw it from the restaurant window. Did they get the license plate number? I saw a dark car, but it came out of nowhere. She had a clear path to cross the street. He must have peeled away from the curb at ninety miles an hour."

"I ran the license plate one of the couples gave us, but it isn't going to do any good."

"Why is that?" Nikki rubbed at her temples as a hammer pounded away inside her head.

"Because it was a diplomat's car. That means the driver has diplomatic immunity, ma'am."

Nikki's knees buckled. The young cop reached out to steady her.

"That means he can't be prosecuted," Nikki said in a choked voice.

"Yes, ma'am, that's exactly what it means."